DON'T
THE MAGIC SHOP !

Peter pressed his face to the window, straining to see into the gloom. Suddenly he froze. Before him, separated only by the thickness of the glass, stood an old, old man, peering with screwed-up eyes right into the boy's startled face. He was grey and deeply wrinkled, his lips drawn back into a nasty leer …

This is the beginning of a spine-tingling adventure for Peter Linton and his friends.

Who is the strange old man in The Magic Shop? What mysterious power does he wield? Why does a visit to The Magic Shop so disturbingly alter the behaviour of Peter's two friends, Harry and Jerry?

It is in a desperate search for answers to such questions that Peter finds himself caught up in a terrifying fight against the forces of Evil. Indeed, it is only through the intervention of the local vicar that Peter and his friends are saved from the clutches of a supernatural enemy and a hideous half-life in the dark eternity of the underworld.

No wonder Peter ends up vowing that he'll never again venture inside a magic shop!

'An exciting – and scary! – story. Thoroughly recommended.'
COLIN DANN
WINNER OF THE NATIONAL AWARD FOR CHILDREN'S LITERATURE.

To Cynthia

DON'T GO NEAR THE MAGIC SHOP !

DEREK DENTON

Jade Publishers
Hazlemere

Jade Publishers
15 Stoatley Rise
Haslemere
Surrey GU27 1AF

First published 1983
First published in Jade Paperbacks 1990

Cover illustration by Gordon King
Cover design by Samantha Edwards

Computer typeset by 'Keyword', Aldbury, Herts
Printed and bound by Cox & Wyman, Reading, Berks

A CIP catalogue record for this book is available
from the British Library

ISBN 0 903461 49 8

CONTENTS

CHAPTER 1

THE OLD SHOP

It was a couple of weeks before school broke up for the Christmas holidays. The wind was in the east, and had been for several days, rocking the tall sycamores on the fringes of the playing fields and tossing the protesting black rooks perilously close to the slate roofs of the Victorian houses that fronted Breckwood Park Drive.

Each morning, Peter Linton would look at the lowering sky and forecast snow for the afternoon; but so far he had been wrong. Harry Sellers, his neighbour and school friend, felt the disappointment just as keenly. Like all boys of their age they longed for the first snowstorm of the winter.

Monday evening found them straggling, disconsolate, up the bleak length of the Drive. The holidays were near but not near enough, and a double helping of maths homework had done nothing to improve the greyness of the day.

"Listen, have we got time to call in at Number Seven?" asked Peter. "I've got a bit of pocket money left and I wouldn't mind getting one of those magic coffins that Steve Corcoran's got."

"Yes, they're good, aren't they? But he didn't buy it at the Magic Shop. His dad got it in town."

"Well, they might have one there. It's worth a try, anyway."

It was an old building; the windows were dark and dusty, and the paint was peeling away from the woodwork. On that late afternoon, when all the other shops in the Drive were a bright glitter of lights, Number Seven looked darker and gloomier than ever.

If any other shop had looked so drab it would never have attracted any customers. But a magic shop was different. The darkness, the silence, the stillness inside, added to its air of mystery; and that, of course, was its stock-in-trade.

Harry flattened his nose against the window-pane. His gaze took in faded yellow boxes of tricks, dusty plastic toys, fly-blown packs of playing cards. At the back of the window space were bottles of strange liquids in oddly shaped containers. As he glanced over the dingy shelves, something in the shadows beyond caught his attention, something that made his heart jump.

Peter was tugging at his arm. "What's the matter? You've gone as white as a sheet."

Harry turned a pale, shocked face towards his companion, but said nothing.

Peter pressed his face to the window, straining to see into the gloom. Suddenly he froze. There before him, separated only by the thickness of the glass, was an old man, peering with screwed-up eyes right into the boy's startled face. He was grey and deeply wrinkled, his lips drawn back into a nasty leer.

The crinkled eyes opened wider and wider, staring and deep, until they were huge, black, hypnotizing orbs. Peter was held by the the unwinking gaze, and sensed the strength of will that lay behind it.

It was Harry's frantic grasp that tore him away. For a second he stood, gasping and dazed, trying to gather his frightened wits, then he took to his heels, careering wildly along the empty pavements with Harry close behind him. It was only when they reached the outskirts of Richmond Park that they stopped for breath.

The shrill notes of the park policeman's whistle sounded through the dark, a warning to any stragglers that it was time for the gates to be closed. Harry and Peter ignored it. Making for a gap in the railings, they squeezed through and plunged into the undergrowth. A couple of minutes later they reached the gang hut.

It was not very large. The boys had built it themselves, using old boards for the walls, and a piece of hardboard laid on a network of dead branches for the roof, the whole structure being bound together by a piece of old tarpaulin draped over the top. Despite its lack of comforts, it was familiar, friendly territory, and Harry and Peter crawled in through the low door with a feeling of relief.

Someone was already there, sitting hunched up in the confined space and trying to warm his hands at a sputtering candle. It was Jerry Potter, the third member of their gang.

It was some time before Jerry could get a word out of either of them, and even when he did, it was obvious he didn't believe their tale.

"Come off it!" he snorted. "You might be able to fool

my kid brother with that story, but surely you don't expect me to fall for it!"

"Jerry, this *isn't* a joke. I didn't really believe any of those stories about the Magic Shop until this evening. But seeing that old man really gave me the creeps." Harry shuddered.

"But I don't see why you two should be behaving as if you had seen a ghost."

"You don't understand," broke in Peter. "There was something evil about him. I ... I can't explain why, but I got the feeling he really wanted to harm us."

Jerry remained unconvinced, but puzzled. Peter did tend to be a little over-imaginative at times, but Harry was generally very level-headed.

"I think I must see this weird character for myself," he said sceptically. "Let's meet at the front gates after school tomorrow, and then we can all pay a visit to the Magic Shop."

Harry, who had been annoyed by his friend's attitude, and was anyway feeling much braver now, agreed immediately. But it took them a long time to persuade Peter.

CHAPTER 2

ACCIDENTS WILL HAPPEN

A cold wind was blowing and Harry and Jerry were dancing with impatience on the edge of the pavement outside the school gates.

"Where is he?" asked Harry for the umpteenth time.

"I don't know. He was right behind me on the stairs. I expect he'll be along any minute. He's probably in the cloakroom now fetching his coat."

Jerry blew on his hands and then rubbed them to get some warmth into them. "I think he's scared and he's gone home. Let's go without him."

Harry frowned. "It's not like him to back out when he's given his word. Shall we give him a few more minutes?"

As he spoke, a single snowflake settled on his collar and the tall sycamore trees behind the sandstone wall of the playground groaned in the wind.

"Oh, come on, Peter! Where are you?" muttered Harry, shivering.

"Time's up," said Jerry. "We'll go without him. He's chickened out.'

Harry said quietly: "You didn't see what he saw. You'd be scared if you had. It was worse for him than for me."

"Rubbish! You imagined it."

"You'll see for yourself soon enough."

The two boys turned away from the school and set off at a brisk pace along the pavement. A sudden flurry of snowflakes whirled in the air and Harry pulled up his collar close about his ears. As they approached Number Seven, the afternoon seemed to grow darker.

Jerry went straight to the window and pressed his freckled nose against the glass, but, to his disappointment, he could see nothing for the condensation running down inside the window.

"Let's go in," he called to Harry. "That's what we came for."

Harry, however, seemed reluctant to make a move, so Jerry pushed past him and grabbed the handle.

Meanwhile, Peter was gazing down in dismay at the pile of books scattered all around him on the floor of the corridor. Then he looked up at the angry face of Mr Roberts, the maths master.

"Why can't you look where you're going, Linton?"

Mr Roberts was known to be a man of spectacular outbursts of temper, though if the truth were known he tried hard to control it. Just at that moment Peter found himself the object of the teacher's bitter scrutiny.

"Well? Aren't you going to pick them up?" Inwardly Mr Roberts was counting to ten slowly.

"Yes, sir. I'm very sorry, sir," stammered Peter, and he began to gather the books. As he did so, he was thinking of the others. They would be at the gates by now, impatient to start.

Mr Roberts watched him with a sort of brooding anger. When Peter gave him the books, he pursed his lips.

"Speeds in excess of 100 miles per hour in the school corridor are forbidden. Do you know that?"

"Yes, sir." His hopes began to rise. Perhaps Mr Roberts wasn't going to be gritty after all.

"What's more, we keep to the left in this school."

"Yes, sir."

Mr Roberts's counting routine was obviously working, for there was the hint of a grim smile on his lips when he added: "You can carry the books down to my car. It's either that or you can write me six million lines."

Peter grinned with relief and then remembered the other two waiting for him. A glance at his watch told him he was already late by a good five minutes.

He followed Mr Roberts along the corridor, wishing he could walk a little faster, but he daren't push too far ahead without giving offence. As they were passing the headmaster's study, Miss Jones, the school secretary, popped her grey head out.

"Oh, Mr Roberts, can you spare a moment? The Head wants a word with you."

Peter groaned inwardly.

"Wait here for me, Linton. I don't suppose the Head will keep me long." And Mr Roberts knocked on the door and went in, leaving Peter alone in the passage with the exercise books.

Peter could do nothing but wait. Mr Walker, the Head, was known to the boys as Walker the Talker, for he never said anything in two words when he could say it in ten.

Peter looked at his watch. It was past four already.

"Come on, sir," he muttered impatiently. "Hurry up."

It was a good quarter of an hour before Mr Roberts emerged from the Head's study.

"Sorry to have kept you waiting for so long, Linton. You'd better run along. Give me the books. I'll carry them myself."

Peter handed over the pile of exercise books and ran off. He was in too much of a hurry to remember to say goodnight to the master.

As he had expected, the other two had gone without him. He looked up the road, but could see no sign of them. He reflected for a moment and then started off along the pavement in the tracks of his friends. All around him snowflakes danced and whirled. He pulled the hood of his anorak close around his ears and ran on past the lighted shop fronts, his feet slipping a little on the wet paving stones. At last he reached Number Seven.

He entered the doorway and stretched out his hand to turn the small brass doorknob. It was only when his fingers actually gripped the metal that he saw the notice behind the dusty glass panel above the handle. It said simply: CLOSED.

His heart fell. He had missed the fun. He was too late. The others were probably at home by now.

All the same, he went to the front of the shop and peered through the glass. The premises were in darkness. All he could make out was a dim red glow somewhere at the back of the shop.

As he stood there in the falling snow, he tried to remember the face he had seen. Perhaps he had imagined it – a trick of the light maybe. Yes, no doubt the others would be wondering what had kept him back. They would probably make fun of him, saying he was too scared to go with them. He bit his lip in annoyance and turned to run down the street in the direction of his home.

By the time he reached Sloan Street, his hair was white with snow, but he went straight to Harry's house and rang the bell.

Mrs Sellers frowned out into the snow. "Is that you, Peter? What a terrible night! My goodness, look at you! You'd better come in."

She stood aside to let him pass, but Peter stayed where he was. He was wondering what Harry would say when he saw him, and he was not looking forward to his friend's scornful greeting.

"I … er … just wondered if Harry was in."

The tall, stout woman looked at him with some surprise.

"No, love. He said he might be home late. He didn't say where he was going, though. I assumed it was something to do with school. In fact I thought it was him when you rang the bell."

Mrs Sellers looked at the snow settling on Peter's shoulders. "Listen," she said, "if you're not coming in, you'd better be off home. You'll catch your death in this weather."

"Yes," said Peter thoughtfully, and took his leave.

But he did not go home. He stood for a moment in the

gateway, chewing his lip and wondering if it was worthwhile trotting to Jerry's house in the next street. However, when he got there, the house was in darkness. He knocked, but knew there was no one in. After waiting in the snow for a full five minutes, he walked away, an uneasy feeling creeping into the pit of his stomach.

CHAPTER 3

NO ESCAPE

The door creaked open and somewhere a bell tinkled faintly. Harry and Jerry moved forward into the long dark room, at the end of which a dim fire glowed in the grate. It was uncannily quiet; even the noise of the traffic outside seemed to have ceased.

Neither boy spoke as he looked around him. On the left ran a counter, a high barrier made of dark wood. Behind it, tiers of shelves rose right up to the ceiling where they were lost in the gloom. It was like no other shop they had ever been in.

With a suddenness that made them jump, a creaking voice called out: "Don't just stand there, Sellers! Give me a hand."

The two boys stared at each other. "He knows your name!" gasped Jerry.

Harry shook his head, unable to speak.

"Give me a hand, boy, I said. Buck up!" The voice had an irritable edge to it.

Harry stared about him into the darkness. "Where are you? I can't see."

"Eyes, laddie. Use your eyes! I'm up here."

Both boys stared about them for the old man they expected to see, but they could see no one.

Now the voice was sharp with impatience: "I do not relish being kept waiting! In fact I have been known to lose my temper!"

"I ... I ... I just can't see you," stammered Harry. "I am trying. Really."

"Then listen carefully. When I say I am up here, I *mean* that I am up here ... *on the shelf* !" The voice had almost reached screaming-pitch.

Suddenly, Jerry pointed with a shaking hand at a large box on the third shelf up behind the counter. "Look!"

It was a wooden box, about four or five feet long and about a foot deep. Over the side of the box flapped a white-gloved hand.

"What shall I do?" whispered Harry to his friend.

"Do? You will give me your hand at once! That's what you'll do."

"Get ready to run," muttered Jerry.

But Harry was approaching the shelf cautiously; and all the time the hand flapped and fluttered, and the voice squawked at him.

Jerry could hardly bear to watch as Harry proffered his fingertips. Immediately, his hand was gripped by the white glove. The boy yelled as he felt the strength of the sinewy fingers through the soft white substance of the glove. When he snatched his hand away, he jerked the box off the shelf, and if fell with a clatter right on top of him.

Jerry was halfway to the door before he was stopped in his flight by hearing his name called imperiously by the voice, this time from the region of the floor behind the

18

counter.

'Potter. Come back here *at once*! And help me *up*! That is an *order*!"

The owner of the voice was clearly in a frightful temper, for each sentence ended in a sort of yelp. Timidly the boy shuffled back towards the counter, looking for Harry.

Harry was lying, dazed, full length on the floor with the box on top of him. As he gathered his wits, the first thing he saw was Jerry's frightened face staring down at him.

"Help me up," muttered Harry, trying to sit upright. But Jerry stepped back as if afraid of him.

Then Harry became aware of the weight across his legs. With a struggle he turned and leaned on one elbow. Straining his eyes in the dark, he saw a sprawling figure with the grotesquely large head of a dwarf staring glassily at him. The mouth sagged open, but the shouting had stopped the instant Harry started to sit up. Now, there was no sound in the room whatsoever.

With a trembling hand Harry reached out and touched the head. It was hard and very cold to the touch. Peering at it more closely, he found himself examining the painted face of a ventriloquist's dummy. His terrified cry as he pushed the thing clear of him and scrambled to his feet frightened Jerry; but any sounds the boys may have made were swamped by waves of high-pitched laughter.

"Oh, dear. I can see," gasped the voice at last, "that you didn't like my little trick! But never mind – I have lots of others."

Jerry had had enough and he ran to the shop door and turned the handle, but the door wouldn't open.

"We can't get out!" he gasped.

"Let me try," said Harry, joining him. "You're right, it's locked!"

"What do we do now?" asked Jerry, fighting back the panic which was swelling in his throat.

"Wait and see," said the voice. "Wait and see."

"It's a record, or there's a hidden microphone," said Harry, trying to sound calm.

"But how do you explain the dummy?" muttered Jerry. "I mean, it grabbed hold of you."

"Yes," rejoined the voice, "how do you explain that, Harry? Tell him."

"Well ... it was a trick ... electronics ... or something."

"Yes. Hee-hee ... or *something*. Hee-hee-hee!" The owner of the voice sounded wildly amused.

The boys now stood back to back peering around.

"If only it wasn't so dark in here, I wouldn't feel so scared," said Jerry,

Immediately, a red flare filled the room with a hideous light like the phosphorescent glow of a coloured firework. As the light died it was replaced by a green flare, and then a blue one.

"Do you like my tricks, boys?"

"Well," said Harry, still trying to be brave, "that's all they are, isn't it? Tricks, I mean."

"Indeed they are. But what tricks! You have never seen the like before. And there are plenty more!"

"We haven't enough money to buy anything fancy," said Jerry trying to pretend things were normal.

"I am not *selling* anything, young Potter. Nothing in this establishment is for sale."

The final flare slowly died, and then they were alone in the darkness. Outside, the last of the winter daylight had faded from the streets. The only source of illumination left was the fire, and that was the merest glow of fading embers. The two boys stood close to each other, straining their ears for the sound of an approaching footstep, or the swish of a curtain perhaps – anything that might herald the arrival of the owner of the voice that had engaged them from the moment they had entered the shop.

Suddenly, from a source that they could not determine, a stark white light seemed to well up until the room was suffused with a glaring brightness, as if the walls themselves were glowing.

"I knew you'd come today," said the voice from immediately behind them. It was a creaking voice, now, with just a hint of brooding in it. "Yes, I knew it would be today. I saw it in my mirror. My mirror shows me everything I need to know."

The speaker was an old man, barely five foot tall. His hair was a dirty white colour and lay straight on his head, in a fringe. He was wearing a skull-cap. His eyes were like two holes in a piece of blank parchment.

"I know all about you," went on the voice, though the old man's lips hardly seemed to move at all; the brown teeth merely grinned at them. "I know where you live, I know your school, I know your favourite lessons, I know your teachers … I even know what sums you got wrong in arithmetic this morning: number thirteen and number twenty- five."

"But how …?"

The only reply to Harry's question was a creaking

laugh.

The old man was dressed in a long black coat that fell from his closely buttoned neck down to his pointed shoes. Small, clawlike hands jutted from his sleeves and rested together on the silver head of a black cane. He surveyed both boys closely before continuing: "Yes, indeed, I knew you were coming here. In search of adventure, I fancy? Well, perhaps you will have it, eh?"

He turned away from them and began to circle the room, his head slightly bowed, his cane tapping on the floorboards. Round and round he went, tapping rhythmically, until Harry and Jerry were half hypnotized watching him. Then he stopped and faced them. He was between them and the door; their retreat was effectively cut off. He began to talk once more.

"In case you're having second thoughts, I should point out, gentlemen, that this will be your one and only chance to embark upon your adventure, your journey, your leap in the dark, shall we say?" His words ended in a rather chilling snigger. "Are you game for a real adventure? Eh, young Potter? What do you say?"

The fact was that Jerry could still remember his own scornful words about Peter being scared, so he was reluctant to say anything that would show how frightened he was. He simply stared back at the old man, biting his lip and hoping that Harry would think of some way to extricate the pair of them from their predicament.

The old man stared at them, his eyes glittering, and his thin shoulders began to shake. As he laughed at them, his head began to wobble, and the more his head wobbled on his thin neck, the wilder his laughter became. Step by slow step the boys retreated till they were pressed back against the counter. They glanced at each other and then back at their tormentor.

In the fraction of time that they had taken their eyes from the old man, he had changed. All that remained of him was the long black coat and the fading outline of his grinning face, dissolving into the air even as they watched. The hands melted away till the cane was left standing upright on its own. They were looking at an empty coat and a silver-headed stick, both suspended in mid-air.

"Take the cane," commanded the old man's voice sharply. "Take the cane, one of you. Whatever you do, do not give it up to anyone."

"Look," stammered Harry, "I … I think we'd like to go home … please."

"Oh, no. I don't think I can allow that. No, indeed, there's no going home for you just now. That wouldn't do at all. Now is the time for your great adventure. After all, that is what you came here seeking."

Harry found the stick thrust into his hands. Then the coat began to turn slowly round and round on the spot, almost as if it were performing the first steps of an ancient dance. Slowly, slowly at first it went, and then it gathered pace until it was spinning madly about the room like a Whirling Dervish.

Suddenly, the light went out.

In the dark, unseen hands plucked at the cane.

Instinctively, Harry clutched it to him, and the next moment he was being dragged roughly about the room. He yelled for help: "Hold on to me, Jerry! Hold on!"

Harsh quarrelling broke out all about them in the

darkness, and there was a violent rushing to and fro in the air above them. The next attack, the stick was torn from Harry's grasp. His cry of terror was matched by another, fainter cry, far off and fading.

As the sound died on the air, light began to leak back into the room. The boys stared about them. They seemed to be quite alone in the shop, and on the floor at their feet lay the coat, now torn to ribbons, and a tuft of what looked like the old man's white hair.

After a moment of shocked silence, Jerry and Harry fled to the door. "Let's get out of here."

The door seemed too flimsy really to separate them so completely from the normal world, the world of shoppers and buses, snowflakes and school, jam bread and football matches; but the door knob just turned and turned in Harry's hand without releasing the catch.

"Try pulling it," urged Jerry, and together they heaved on the door, but to no avail. "Then we'll shout for help. We've got to do *something* to get out of here."

So they shouted, at the tops of their voices. But as they yelled, a fierce wind sprang up and howled around the building, shaking the door till it rattled.

"Did you hear that?" asked Jerry, his eyes large with fright.

They called again, but the moment they opened their mouths to call for help, the gale swooped down on the building, making the old shop shudder and vibrate.

"We're trapped!" gasped Jerry. "We're never going to get out of here."

"Oh yes we are! Give me a hand," said Harry, a determined look in his eye. "We'll smash the window and

24

get out that way."

Together they knocked aside the dusty boxes on the shelves at the back of the window, tore away some of the shelving and, with Harry's aid, Jerry climbed into the window space. Packs of cards were crushed underfoot, tricks scattered, masks crumpled.

"Give me that piece of shelving, Harry. I'm going to smash my way out of it."

He swung the wood and struck the glass a heavy blow, but it did not break. Instantly he dropped the timber and held his hand to his mouth, sucking his fingers, his face screwed up with pain.

"What's wrong?" asked Harry.

"Try it and you'll find out," said Jerry, nursing his injured hand.

"Right, move over," said Harry, taking the wood and climbing up beside Jerry.

He aimed a shattering blow at the glass. Where the wood touched the window, a crackle of flame licked at the timber and he felt an agony run like fire through his hands and wrists and up his arms, making him scream with pain.

"You're wasting your time," said the voice of the old man behind them. He was very calm now. "Come along. You will come to no harm if you do as I direct you."

"Where is he?" whispered Harry, looking round.

"Time is slipping by. I want you to go to the fireplace and stand there." The voice was quiet but insistent.

Reluctantly the boys obeyed, scrambling down from the window space and returning to the hearth, where the old man suddenly appeared. What had, yesterday, seemed a splendid chance for adventure, had now taken on a

25

nightmare aspect. Their boyish prank had ballooned into something too big for them to cope with.

"On the mantlepiece is a small metal box. Open it. In it there is a powder. I want you to sprinkle it over the embers. Stand well back and hold your breath for a count of fifty. Don't argue. Just do it. You will hear me counting."

Harry and Jerry exchanged uncertain glances. At last, after a bit of fumbling in the gloom, Harry reached up and found the box. With a flick of his thumb he opened it. A strong stench of decay filled his nostrils. Holding it away from him, Harry took a deep breath and emptied the contents of the tin on to the fire.

At once the embers glowed white hot. The boys tried to look away, but something forced them to gaze deep into the heart of the fire, which seemed to be expanding.

Dimly they were aware of a voice counting the slow throb of their pulses. One … two … three … four …

Already they were finding it hard to hold their breath as the voice had instructed. The blood was pounding in their ears by the time thirty was reached, so slowly did the count proceed.

The voice droned on and on. Thirty-five … thirty-six … thirty-seven …

A faint noise distracted Harry's attention from the fire and, as he peered into the gloom, he saw the old man dragging a long cheval mirror towards the fireplace.

A disturbing buzzing filled the air. Harry shook his head to clear it. All thought of holding his breath had vanished from his mind; all he was aware of now was that buzzing and a desire to close his eyes and float off to sleep.

Suddenly, he was wide awake, roused by a startled cry from Jerry. The old man had positioned the mirror so that it was facing the fireplace, and he stood there bowing and smiling in a mocking sort of way, and gesturing as if to say: *"Behold what I have here!"*

Through the fumes that had begun to thicken in the air as the fire died down, the boys stared, with increasing amazement, at their own reflections in the tall mirror. First one and then the other reflection bowed and saluted them. There was a Harry nodding and smiling at them from the glass, and there was Jerry, too.

An awful terror gripped Harry, for he could see at once that these reflections had a life of their own. Both he and Jerry were standing perfectly still; neither of them was bowing or waving like those figures beyond the glass.

What was happening to them?

Suddenly, the answer no longer seemed important. A wave of intense weariness engulfed them both; all that mattered was the weight of their eyelids. But just before Harry's eyes closed, he was almost certain that he saw his own reflection step forward into the room from beyond the glass. For one shimmering instant he saw the surface of the mirror part like the waters of a pool as the boy passed through to stand beside the grinning old man.

"It can't be true! It *can't* be true," he muttered, as if on the fringes of a dream.

When next he opened his eyes, the fire was almost out, but there was something odd about it. He could not work it out at first. Then, as his brain cleared, he realized that he was not looking into the back of the grate as before: he was looking into a room.

"Is that the shop we're looking at?" asked Jerry, sounding sleepy and puzzled.

"It must be. Look, there's the door we entered by."

"Yes, and the broken shelving."

They looked at one another.

"Then where are we now? Have we come through the fire?"

"Yes," said Jerry, looking around him in wonderment, "we must have."

And from far away came the sound of an old man's mocking laughter ...

CHAPTER 4

SOMETHING STRANGE
IS GOING ON

Peter sat staring at his plate; the food on it had hardly been touched.

"What's the matter with you, Peter? You off your food?"

Peter looked up at his brother, Les. "I'm not hungry," he muttered.

"Well, pass it over here."

"No," cut in Mrs Linton. "Peter, you're a growing lad and you need good food inside you to help you grow." After a moment's uneasy silence, Mrs Linton looked at her younger son and said: "What's the matter, Peter?

"Honestly, Mum, it's nothing."

How could he say he was worrying about his pals? The whole story would seem so trivial. What was so odd about being late for an appointment and missing a bit of fun? Harry and Jerry had probably gone on somewhere else when they had found Number Seven closed. They might even have met some other boys and gone off with them. And yet he could not shake off the feeling of unease that was spoiling his appetite.

He was still toying with his food when his mother said sharply: "Now you eat up! There are plenty of children in China and India who would be only too pleased to eat that ham."

"You always say that, Mum," observed Les, winking at Peter.

Peter sighed and ate a mouthful of food.

When Peter had moped around the house for half an hour or so after tea, his mother said: "For heaven's sake, why don't you call on Harry and see what he's doing? You're getting on my nerves."

So Peter put on his coat and ran down the street. As he rang the bell of Harry's house, he glanced at his watch. It was eight o'clock. Harry should be home by now.

Mrs Sellers opened the door. "Come in, Peter. I suppose you want to see Harry, though why anyone should bother with him, the mood he's in, I don't know."

Peter followed her into the living-room and found his friend sprawled in a chair watching television.

"Hello, Harry. Sorry I missed you. How did you get on?"

"We didn't get in. The place was closed."

Peter nodded. "It was closed when I got there, too. I ran into Mr Roberts and knocked his books flying. He kept me back. That's why I was late."

Harry said nothing. As yet he hadn't bothered to look at Peter, but had continued to watch the television programme.

Mrs Sellers moved across to the set and switched it off. "Harry, your friend is talking to you. It's bad manners to watch television when you have visitors. I've told you often enough."

For answer Harry grunted and got to his feet.

"Now where are you going?" asked his mother.

"I'm going to bed. Any objections?"

Mrs Sellers looked surprised and then angry. "Don't you talk to me like that. You're not too big to get smacked, remember. Now sit down and be sociable. I'll go and make a cup of tea. I'm sure you'd like one, wouldn't you, Peter?"

"Well, if you don't mind …"

Harry turned a hostile gaze on Peter.

"What's up with you, Harry?" asked Peter.

Harry said nothing. He simply walked to the door and left the room. Peter was still standing looking at Mrs Sellers when he heard the bedroom door slam.

"Peter, I'm so sorry. I've *never* seen him behave like that. He's been in a funny mood ever since he came in. I haven't had a civil word out of him. I don't know what's got into him."

"Nor me," said Peter.

"You haven't been fighting, have you?"

"No. I told you: I was late because I bumped into Mr Roberts. I can't think that would make him so bad-tempered though. It just isn't like him."

Mrs Sellers sighed. "Well, I'll just go and make that cup of tea anyway. I could do with one."

"Thanks, Mrs Sellers, but not for me. I think I'd better be going."

Harry's mother looked embarrassed but didn't try to detain him. At the door she said:

"He'll be over it in the morning. He's sure to be."

Peter stepped out into the snow and said goodnight. He wasn't in the mood to go home just at the moment, so he went for a walk along the silent streets. The snow was a good four inches deep by now and it muffled the usual city noises. Even the clatter from the shunting yards on the far side of the allotments seemed to be missing.

Almost before he realized where he was going, he was approaching the street where the Magic Shop was. He stared at it from the opposite side of the road for a couple of minutes, but there was nothing exceptional to see. The windows were dark and uninviting, but that was all. So, after staring at the shop for a few minutes more, he turned miserably for home.

It was a long time before Peter finally drifted off to sleep that night. He heard Les arriving home on his motorbike and later, when he had put the machine away in the shed at the back of the house, he heard him creeping upstairs to bed. Les had long since started to snore his way round the Silverstone circuit before Peter's eyelids drooped. When he finally did sleep, he dreamed of the Magic Shop and the old man's face scowling at him.

After breakfast the next morning, he felt tempted not to call for Harry. He did call, nevertheless.

Mrs Sellers's broad friendly face peered at him round the door. She was not an early riser and she was wearing her red dressing-gown as usual. As she spoke, she fingered a stray wisp of hair into place.

"He's gone on ahead, Peter. I just don't know what's got into him. He didn't even wait for his breakfast."

"Oh," said Peter, turning away, dispirited.

"Are you *sure* you two haven't had an argument about something?"

"Quite sure. Everything was fine until yesterday evening."

She shrugged. "Well, I just thought it might explain his behaviour. Hey, you'd better be on you way or you'll be late."

Peter turned once more and trudged off along the snowy pavements of Sloan Street. The last thing he wanted just then was to catch up with Harry.

When he arrived at school, he went straight into the small yard behind the gym where he, Harry and Jerry always met before school. As he rounded the corner, he saw Harry talking to Jerry over on the far side of the yard. When he headed for them, they turned and walked rapidly off. He called, but they ignored him. He felt his cheeks redden with annoyance, but his pride would not let him run after them. He bitterly resented the fact that they had not given him the chance to talk things over with them.

He looked forlornly around at the wet expanse of slush that the many feet had churned up. Old Froggy, the Deputy Head, would confine them all to school during the morning break in view of what he called "the inclement weather". It was a pity, because a good snow-fight would have helped to relieve his feelings somewhat.

The nine o'clock bell rang and the boys began to troop into school.

CHAPTER 5

PERIL BY TWILIGHT

"I don't like the way he laughs," said Jerry. "It's as though he's enjoying some joke at our expense."

Harry nodded his agreement.

"He's sort of sly, like Mr Savage in the sweet-shop. You know, always a penny short in your change hoping you won't notice."

Harry didn't speak because he was looking around for some sign of the fireplace, but there was none. At last he said: "We must be at the back of the shop somewhere, but look at that wall. It's solid rock. There's nothing like that in Number Seven."

The two boys prodded the wall with their hands and kicked at it with their feet. It was undoubtedly rock: no tricks this time.

"Then how did we get here? I mean, there should be a hole for the grate.'

"Come on. Let's have a good look round for it."

As they moved slowly along the wall, examining it, Jerry said: "Hey, have you noticed anything?"

"What?"

"It's light in here. But where is the light coming from?"

Both boys turned and stared.

"It's like a sort of cave, isn't it? Except that the wall on this side has been straightened out." Harry lifted his head and shouted at the top of his voice: "Oi-oi!"

The sound leapt back off the rock surface with the liveliness of a pack of rubber balls: "Oi-oi-oi-oi-oi-oi-oi."

"Listen to that," breathed Jerry. And he shouted: "Down with school!"

"... with school -ool -ool -ool -ool -ool!" came the echo.

They half expected to hear the old man's laughter once again, but the only thing mocking them was the sound of their own words.

"The light seems to be coming from along there. Let's have a look," suggested Harry.

The cave, or passage, narrowed rapidly until it was only just wide enough for them to pass through. Moving carefully along, they emerged at the bottom of a flight of rough-hewn steps which led up to an oval of light. At the top of the stairs they walked out into the blinding rays of a huge golden sun which was setting in a blaze in the western sky. They stood there for a moment, stunned by the sight of distant hills blackening against the sun as it sank steadily towards them.

There was no snow here, and the air was warm. But the faint blush of purple which hinted at the coming twilight also heralded the oncoming chill of night.

"There's a path going down through those trees," said Jerry, pointing further along the bluff on which they stood. The entrance to their cave was some hundred or so feet above a plain, and behind them the cliff rose sheer to a crest three hundred feet up.

"It looks a bit steep," said Harry. "Do you think we'll be able to manage it?"

"We'll have to if we want to get down from here."

"I suppose we've got no option, then. Let's have a good look at the view first. Can you see any signs of civilization?"

The plain below was barren for a distance of about a mile and a half; then trees began to populate the flat land, sporadic at first and then crowding closer together till they appeared to form a dense barrier stretching away as far as the eye could see.

To the west, there was a pale gleam of distant water. It was hard to tell whether it was a lake or a wide river.

"Where do you think we are?" asked Jerry.

Harry shrugged. He had an uneasy feeling that this place wasn't anywhere they had ever heard of.

"What's my mum going to say when I don't come home tonight?" said Jerry, a sudden catch in his voice. "She'll be worried stiff."

Harry said nothing. The same thought had been troubling him for some time

Jerry broke the ensuing silence. "Is that a castle over there?" he asked, pointing towards a distant landmark.

"I suppose it could be," Harry agreed with growing excitement.

Standing there on the edge of the cliff, looking out across that alien landscape, they were both filled with a terrible loneliness.

"Do we camp here for the night, or make for that castle and ask for shelter?" said Jerry.

"I fancy the castle rather than staying here in this cave. It's bound to get cold once the sun goes down."

"We'd better make a start, then. The path's a bit steep here below the cave, but it seems to get easier further along." And so saying, Jerry slithered down the first few feet of the path where it left the small ledge outside the cave.

It took them ten minutes to scramble down to the plain. Then, fixing their eyes on the distant castle, they set off to the north.

"It should take us about an hour, all being well," said Harry moving steadily forward beside his friend.

The sun was now a huge red disc sliding down behind the hills to their left. Daylight would not remain for much longer, and both boys knew it. They quickened their pace.

They had covered about three-quarters of a mile when Jerry stopped abruptly. "What was that?"

Before Harry could answer, there floated on the air a distant howling. It seemed to rise up out of the forest away to their right, eerie and chilling.

The boys looked at each other; neither liked to say what the sound had reminded him of, but each could see the dark fear in the other's eyes.

Ahead of them rose the battlements and turrets of the castle, the last of the sun's rays glowing weakly on the sheer faces of its towers. A banner floated high above the keep, and, unseen by the boys, a figure moved on the battlements.

"Let's get a move on," said Harry breaking into a trot.

They had gone scarcely fifty yards when Jerry stooped to remove a stone from his shoe. It was then that they caught the faint high piping of a whistle, three distinct notes cleaving the gathering dusk. Both boys saw the flicker of movement to their right.

"Dogs!" shouted Harry. "Look, dogs!"

There was a small pack of them some hundred yards off. The animals had stopped and were watching them, their ears pricked and their noses sniffing the air.

"They're big, aren't they? I don't like the look of them." As he spoke, Jerry looked for a stone to throw.

From the ground a deep purple dusk seemed to be rising and blurring the shapes of things, so that it was difficult to see the animals in any detail.

Again there sounded three notes, a different sequence this time, and the dogs immediately fanned out.

"Look," gasped Harry, "over there on the left! More of them. Let's keep moving. Come on!" And they trotted on towards the castle, hoping that the dogs would keep their distance.

They were among trees now. They were sparse and did not hinder their progress, but the dogs were still closing in on them.

"Get a stick," said Jerry halting to fling the stone he had been carrying at a huge dog that had come up closer than the rest. He missed his aim but the rattle of the pebble against a tree trunk turned the beast aside to rejoin the pack where it stood watching them.

Jerry found two stout sticks and he passed one to his friend. "I'm not sure these *are* dogs. They're too big. Look at that one over there! It's massive."

It was easy to see what Jerry meant. The animal in question was bigger than any alsation Harry had ever seen.

Even as they stared at it, the beast threw back its head and howled.

"They couldn't be … no, there aren't any left in England nowadays … are there?" said Harry.

"Wolves? No. But who said this was England?"

Once more a whistle sliced the air, clear and high, and once more the animals moved forwards, forcing the boys on towards the fortress.

Jerry picked up another stone and flung it, but it did little to stop the pursuit. Harry's aim was a little better and there was a brief scattering among the animals, but they soon closed in again.

"D'you know what?" said Harry.

"What?"

"They're near enough to rush us, and yet they haven't tried it."

"Yes, but they will."

As if on cue, a single clear note floated through the evening air and once more the pack advanced on them, not running, but trotting faster than before, with the animals on either flank moving forward to form a semi-circle round the boys.

"Come on," cried Harry, grabbing hold of Jerry's arm. "Let's make a dash for it. We'll be finished otherwise. Keep your stick handy."

Jerry didn't need telling. He was away in a flash, feet flying lightly over the ground, with Harry not far behind.

After them swept the dogs, like a dark sinister tide moving over the land. The fleeing boys could hear the snapping and snarling of the pack and it unnerved them.

Ahead, the massive bulk of the castle reached out of the

gloom, but its steep stone walls offered little sign of welcome. The gates, a sombre frame set in the smooth dark stone, remained firmly closed. But the gasping boys raced on, their arms flailing the air as they covered the last few yards to the fortress. Finally, by the unyielding castle gates, the boys turned to face the animals.

Teeth flashing and hackles raised, the pack was closing in. Jerry lashed out viciously with the stick and felt it connect with a snout. There was a furious snarling as the leading animals tumbled over each other in a tangle of threshing bodies. An instant later, however, they were up again, poised for the next attack.

At the same moment a series of sharp, staccato notes pierced the air like musical tracer bullets. The animals turned in their tracks and fell back, forming a semi-circle round the boys, menacing but immobile.

Harry and Jerry barely had time to realize that the immediate danger had abated, when a small door let into the main gate swung open. They didn't need anyone to invite them through.

CHAPTER 6

THE CASTLE

There was no sign of the person who had opened the gate; no one to thank, no one to explain their presence to. They were quite alone. Looking around, they realized they were in the outer bailey, the wide space between the castle's inner and outer fortifications. It was like a dark canyon, empty of all life.

Seventy yards away rose the grim defences of the main fortress, and set in a double tower was the gateway. Very nervously, they crossed the outer bailey and, with beating hearts, walked in under the arch and along the tunnel-like passage.

They had gone about ten paces when the low archway behind them vibrated heavily with the rumbling of a stout portcullis crashing down, cutting off their retreat. Hardly had the grille ceased shaking from its impact, when a second framework began to descend from the archway ahead, rolling its grumbling sound across the air towards them.

"Come on!" yelled Harry, punching Jerry's shoulder and sprinting for the exit. They flung themselves forward under the second grille with less than a foot to spare.

Having recovered their breath a little, they began to take stock of their surroundings, expecting all the time to see some sign of the occupants of the castle.

They were in a large courtyard, presumably the inner bailey, the heart of the fortress. On all sides there were tall windows, but no lights within. Above the windows of the great keep ran a crenellated walk-way, where sentries might have patrolled. But there was no one there.

In the centre of the courtyard stood a well. They peered cautiously over the edge but it was getting too dark to see anything. Harry picked up a pebble and dropped it down the shaft and began counting. After what seemed an age there still had been no splash nor any other sound.

"It can't be *that* deep!" he said to Jerry.

He tried another stone, a bigger one this time. This one struck against the side of the wall. After a pause it struck again, and then again and again until all sound died away.

"It *can't* be bottomless, surely?"

Jerry was about to reply when his attention was drawn away to the battlements where a flaming torch had appeared. Another torch came into view, and yet another, until the courtyard was ringed with lights.

From the direction of the gate-house a voice shouted: "There's no one here in the tunnel!"

"They're here – by the well," answered another voice from the roof of the great keep.

The boys looked up – into the staring eyes of a group of men and women.

Harry swallowed nervously and began: "We were chased by dogs across the plain. We came here for shelter. We are lost."

If he expected an answer, he was disappointed. His voice echoed faintly against the walls and then there was silence. The torches flared, the shadows danced, but the spectators remained motionless.

"What now?" asked Harry in a hoarse whisper to Jerry.

"I don't know, but I'm beginning to wish I was back in the cave. I've a feeling we shouldn't have come here."

"Well, we are here, and we can't do anything about it right now."

It was eerie standing there in the gloom, the only light coming from the flickering torches held in the hands of the castle people.

"They're dressed strangely, aren't they?" whispered Jerry. "See? They're all wearing cloaks and sort of togas underneath … like Nero in that film of the television last week."

As they studied the faces that were looking down at them, they noticed there was not one single old person among them. Each one was beautiful in a terrible sort of way, devoid of emotion, ghostlike in the wavering torchlight.

A door slammed massively in the shadows. Footsteps beat a regular rhythm on the stone flags. Round a corner on their left came someone bearing a torch aloft. At the sight of him both boys took a step back.

The man was huge: seven feet tall at least, and heavily muscled. His head was completely devoid of hair, so that the jagged scar, running across his scalp and on down through his left eyebrow to his cheek, stood out in a white ridge which gleamed in the torchlight.

The boys watched with frightened eyes as this giant came towards them. He was wearing loose-fitting breeches made of some animal skin, and stout Roman sandals. Above the waist he was bare, except for a black leather belt running up over one shoulder. Another belt, round his middle, was looped to the first one and acted as the anchor-point for a broad scabbard.

As he came near, the boys shrank back till they were hard up against the wall of the courtyard. Ten feet away from them, the giant stopped and spread his arms out wide. He fixed his eyes unwaveringly on Jerry. Moving slowly, arms still extended, he closed in.

With a cry Jerry started to his left, but an arm swept out and lifted him effortlessly into the air. All Jerry's kicks achieved was a faint grunt of displeasure from the man as he stooped to lay down his torch on the flagstones. Then, holding him aloft at arm's length, the giant strode over to the well.

Harry, rooted to the spot with fear, saw his friend squirming and kicking, heard him squealing with terror as he was held out over the shaft of the well, the giant hands grasping his jacket collar and the seat of his trousers. Suddenly the powerful hands opened and Jerry's body plummeted into the blackness. His scream echoed throughout the courtyard.

Sickness, terror, and disgust swept over Harry. He looked up, through a haze of sweat and tears, at the battlements and the people watching there. He was horrified to see on each handsome face a fixed wooden smile, a mockery of laughter. If this was pleasure, then this world was mad.

"Lucan!" called a faint voice from above. "Take the other one. We'll have him in the well, too."

The giant turned stiffly, and for the first time Harry noticed something odd about the way he held himself. There was an awkward stiffness about the set of the massive shoulders. Instead of being able to turn his head easily and smoothly, like a normal man, the giant had to turn his whole body toward the battlements. He stood, staring up at the torchlight as though hypnotised.

Harry, too, looked up at the pale faces. For all the emotion they now showed, they might have been dummies. A hand fluttered, a sort of signal to the giant, and that was the only movement.

The giant was lurching towards Harry, and the boy moved shakily away from him along the wall. His limbs seemed to have lost their power. Suddenly his foot struck something and he glanced down. It was the stick Jerry had dropped. He snatched it up and held it in both hands.

Lucan stopped and eyed him cautiously before shuffling forward again.

"Why don't you do something?" yelled the boy, looking up at the watchers. "Stop him, please! What have I ever done to you?"

And then, with a sudden surge of determination, he ran. He reached the gate by which he had entered, but the portcullis was still down. There was no way out there.

The giant had retrieved his flaming torch, and in its flickering light, he looked more grotesque than ever as he lumbered across the courtyard.

"At least," muttered Harry, "he's no runner."

But this observation almost brought disaster to Harry, for with a sudden lunge Lucan was at him, thrusting the firebrand towards his head. Harry stumbled as he warded it off with his stick, the sparks flying upwards into the night sky. As he fell, he rolled away from the reaching fingers and was up and away in one flowing movement; but the stick was gone from his grasp. There was no time to pick it up again

As he fled from the gate-house, he was aware of a weird sound from aloft, and he raised his eyes briefly to see the figures on the walkway swaying drunkenly to and fro. The excited chattering of the watchers swelled rapidly into the shouts of an arena crowd. They were calling out in a language that he had never heard before, and yet he seemed to understand every word that they uttered. He heard their taunts and jests and knew what they were … And suddenly Lucan was there.

The giant stood close, arms stretched wide, the torch in his left hand extending the barrier almost another three feet. As Harry ducked, he saw the flames swoop towards him and he pulled back, cowering away. Finally, there was nowhere else to go. The wall was at his back and the giant Lucan was directly before him.

Just then, a piercing whistle-blast screamed through the dark. Lucan froze, arms still spread wide, a grotesque statue illuminated by the dancing yellow flames of the torch in his massive hand. To his right appeared a small, thin young man dressed entirely in black. He, like the watchers above, wore a sort of toga. On his head was a wreath of black laurel-shaped leaves, and he carried a long ebony staff with a silver top shaped like a skull. Round his neck, on a silver chain, hung a silver pentangle which he fingered pensively as he studied Harry with expressionless, dark eyes.

"Please," begged Harry, his voice quavering, "make him leave me alone! I'm not a thief or anything bad like that. I just wanted shelter, and I'll go right away if you want me to. But please don't let him touch me."

The young man's face twitched slightly, and the hideous smile that formed on his face frightened Harry almost as much as Lucan did.

Without speaking, the young man raised an imperious finger and beckoned to someone in the shadows beyond. Two men ran up at a trot and grabbed hold of the trembling boy, taking one arm each in a vice-like grip.

"Take him." The young man's voice was thin, brittle, frail almost. When he spoke, his chest seemed to heave as though he was making a great effort.

The men dragged Harry across the courtyard. He tried to struggle and dig in his heels, but they simply heaved him after them, with Lucan bringing up the rear, lumbering heavily over the flagstones.

By the time they reached the well the sound of shouting had swelled to a roar that sent echoes flying across the still night air.

"In with him," said the young man, his voice suddenly

strong and firm.

Lucan came forward and took the boy from the others. As he was lifted high in the air, Harry made a last desperate effort to struggle free, but to no avail. The giant opened his huge fingers and dropped him over the edge of the well.

With a rush the blackness engulfed him, and he felt himself falling ... falling ... falling ...

CHAPTER 7

THOSE WITHOUT SHADOW

Peter tried hard not to let his friends' behaviour get him down, but he could not stop thinking about it. Both Harry and Jerry snubbed him at school on all possible occasions; in fact it was so noticeable that some of the other boys commented on it. He no longer bothered to call for Harry in the mornings, and he never went near the gang hut.

Eventually his mother said to him: "Have you fallen out with Harry?"

"No, but he's fallen out with me by the look of it." And he told her what had happened.

"Well, I think he's being rather mean about the whole thing. I never thought he was that sort of boy."

"They won't even talk to me. They just walk off when they see me coming."

"In that case I'll have a word with his mother."

"No!" said Peter hastily. "Please don't, Mum. Just leave it, will you?"

Mrs Linton looked at him shrewdly for a moment then suggested: "You can always make new friends. There are plenty of other fish in the sea. All the same, it is a pity. You've been pals for so long."

The real trouble, however, was that Peter's pride had been wounded. He felt he had been wrongly accused and found guilty. But he was puzzled, too. There was something about Harry, and Jerry too, that he felt was odd. It wasn't just their behaviour; there was something else, but he could not say exactly what.

The following day Peter overheard his mother talking to Mrs Sellers. "I can't understand it all. They've always been such good friends."

"Well," said Mrs Sellers a little awkwardly, "I must admit our Harry's been a bit strange recently. He never speaks unless he's spoken too. And you know what a chatterbox he usually is."

After a pause, Mrs Sellers continued: "What really puzzles me is that, whenever he is at home, he locks himself away in his room and does his homework – or so he says. He never was much of a one for homework. I used to have to prise him away from the television every evening in the old days. I suppose I shouldn't complain, but it just doesn't seem natural – not for him. I'd rather have him as his old cheeky self, Mrs Linton. Really I would!"

"Well, perhaps, he's just going through a difficult stage at the moment. Growing up is not always easy. He'll probably be back to normal in a few weeks."

Peter felt his heart lighten, because he was not the only one to sense a difference in Harry. Harry's mother had noticed it too. If only he could pinpoint what it was.

It was on the day following this conversation that Peter was approached by Brian Smith, a fat boy in the same class.

"Have you and Harry had a fight?" he asked.

Peter shook his head.

"But you don't go around together any more, do you?"

Peter said nothing. He was wondering what this was leading to.

"What I mean is … well, you know him better than anyone in this class, don't you? I mean, he's always been a decent sort, wouldn't you say?"

Peter nodded. He didn't want to be drawn on this particular topic.

The other boy hesitated a moment, then seemed to come to a decision.

"I think he's changed." He watched Peter carefully for his reaction, and when he saw Peter's eyes quicken with interest, he went on: "He seems really spiteful these days, and I even saw him battering little Podge Murphy in the yard after school last night."

Peter's eyebrows shot up. Bullying was something Harry would never contemplate.

"What did you do about it?"

"Me?" said Brian, blinking. "What could I do? There were two of them. Potter was with him. Anyway, you know I can't fight."

Peter looked thoughtful, but said nothing.

After a pause, Brian said: "Well, I just thought you might like to know."

"No," snapped Peter, "what you really want to know is whether I've fallen out with Harry because he's changed."

Brian lowered his eyes. "I was only wondering. There's no harm in that, is there? Anyway, listen: do you know he was the only one to hand in homework for old Dodds? *No one* ever does homework for art! And Harry of all people!"

"I see what you mean. Still, I heard Mr Dodds wasn't too pleased with it. Do you know why?"

"I don't, but he got really angry and tore it up. I saw him stuffing the pieces into the basket. He was muttering something about impertinence; said if there was any more of it he'd send for Mrs Sellers."

"Really?"

"Honestly!"

Peter made as if to walk away, but the other boy stopped him.

"There's something else about Harry – and Jerry, too. Harry's right-handed isn't he? And Jerry uses his left."

"Go on."

"Well, you watch them. Harry is using his left hand and Jerry is using his right. Now what about that?"

"Are you sure?" Peter was incredulous.

"You don't have to take my word for it. Just watch them this afternoon in English. You'll see."

As if on cue, the school bell began to ring and the boys trudged in from the playground.

Later that day Peter found Brian in the school library, where he was on duty as a monitor.

"Was I right?" asked Brian.

Peter nodded. "I wasn't sure I believed you in the yard, but I do now. I can't see any reason for it. Can you?"

Brian beckoned him to a bay between the shelves. Reaching up he took down a book from the top shelf and tapped it with his pudgy forefinger. "I've been doing some reading."

"What about?"

"Well, I'm not sure it makes sense."

"Try me. I'll tell you if it doesn't."

"It's this book. It's a collection of short stories about ghosts, and there's one here about a *doppelgänger*."

"A what?"

"A sort of ghost. Anyway, in this story a man is haunted by his double, and it's a sure sign of death for anyone to see his own double. The story is a bit complicated with mirrors and things."

"Mirrors?"

"Yes. The *doppelgänger* is the man's reflection taken from a mirror, and the sure way of telling a *doppelgänger* is to see it in front of a mirror."

"Pardon me if I seem thick, but I don't get it."

"Well, if a *doppelgänger* is a man's image, it can't have a reflection of its own, can it? So, if it passes in front of a mirror, there's no image in the glass. See?"

"Yes, but what's this got to do with Harry and Jerry?"

"Think about it. If you stand in front of a mirror, and raise your right hand, which hand does your reflection hold up?"

Peter screwed up his eyes, picturing it happening.

"It'll be your left," prompted Brian.

"You mean the image's left."

"Yes, that's it, the image's left hand."

"So?"

"So a man's *doppelgänger* will be left-handed if the man is right-handed, and the other way round if he's left-handed."

"Ah, now I understand! You think Harry Sellers isn't

53

Harry Sellers but his *doppelgänger*, right?"

Brian was nodding enthusiastically.

"Do you know what I think, Brian?"

"What?"

"I think you're daft. You'll be telling me next that you believe in vampires."

Brian looked impatient, and for a moment Peter thought he was going to walk away in a huff, but he turned back suddenly and said: "You've seen both of them this afternoon. You know I'm right about the hands, don't you?"

"Yes, but ..."

"Listen, I'll tell you a bit more. After reading those stories I began, just for fun, to watch various people. I was pretending I was a ghost hunter, like one of the men in the story. Anyway, I happened to remember that the only left-hander in the class is Jerry. Everybody knows Jerry is the Junior Eleven's left arm medium-pace bowler."

"Well? So what?" demanded Peter.

"Well, I didn't really expect to see anything different and I didn't."

"But I thought ..."

"I didn't – *at first*. One afternoon everyone was normal; the next morning, I saw Jerry writing with his right hand. I gave him a poke and asked him if he'd hurt his other hand, but he just scowled. Then I noticed Harry was using his left hand."

Peter was silent, trying to think of some reason why the change of hands could have taken place. Was it a bet Harry and Jerry were having as to who could write with his other hand the longest? It wasn't impossible. Contests like that help to break the monotony of school. On one occasion he had counted nine hundred and thirty-eight raindrops on one classroom window during a geography lesson.

"Did you have a look at his writing? Because when you write with your wrong hand, your handwriting is usually terrible. You just can't help it."

Brian was nodding his agreement. "Jerry's was as neat as anything. So was Harry's. They weren't writing slowly, either."

"It certainly is odd," commented Peter, chewing the edge of his lip as he turned things over in his mind.

"That's not all," said Brian excitedly. "I began to watch them carefully after that. I wanted to see if they had shadows."

Suddenly, a tall red-faced boy thrust his head between them. "If you two *must* talk, do you mind going elsewhere. The rest of us would like some peace."

Brian apologized somewhat impatiently, then, turning to Peter, said: "I'll ask Mr Cray if I can leave early. He won't mind, because I did an extra duty during the lunch hour. I'll tell you the rest of it on the way home."

"I'll meet you in the foyer, but don't be long," muttered Peter, and he walked away.

As they walked along, Brian Smith told the rest of his tale.

"I thought I was seeing things at first, but there was no doubt about it. Those two were the only ones in the yard who had no shadow. It was cold yesterday, but the sun was bright."

Peter nodded, remembering. Could this, he wondered, have anything to do with Harry's visit to Number Seven?

It was only after Harry and Jerry had been to The Magic Shop that they had begun to behave oddly towards him.

"Listen, Brian, I want to tell you something, but you must promise not to mention it anyone else just yet." Peter told him about the visit to the Magic Shop, about missing the other two and about Harry's odd behaviour ever since.

"Do you think something happened to them in the Magic Shop, something that changed them?" Brian's eyes grew wide as his thoughts tumbled on in a rush: "Do you think the real Harry and Jerry are still in the Magic Shop and these two are their *doppelgängers*?"

This was going too far and too fast for Peter. "Well, I really hadn't reached that conclusion, Brian. I mean to say ... well, perhaps it's not impossible."

"Listen," said the plump boy earnestly, "we don't know what is possible. This is the supernatural we're talking about and you just can't tell ..."

Peter interrupted him. "Look, let's take one thing at a time, shall we? I agree, you've spotted the change of hands, and I've seen it, too, now. You say they have no shadows, but I haven't seen that yet. I suggest we check on the shadows tomorrow, if we get a chance. What do you say?"

They agreed to meet in the playground in the lunch-break the next day to keep an eye on the other two, and, what was more, to pray for sunshine.

CHAPTER 8

LOOKING FOR PROOF

Brian and Peter met as arranged after lunch. There was no sign of the other two in the main yard where all the football was going on.

"The small yard?" suggested Peter.

As they rounded the corner, they saw both Jerry and Harry sitting in the doorway leading to the woodwork shop. They were talking quietly to one another, but at the sight of Peter and Brian, the conversation ceased abruptly.

Steeling himself for the encounter, Peter approached. "Hello, you two. What are you doing with yourselves these days? I haven't seen you around much."

The other two just stared for a long ten seconds and then Harry replied, rather frostily: "What do you mean? You see us every day in class."

"I meant after school."

There was no reply to this, so Brian said: "They're playing soccer in the other yard. Do you fancy a game?"

Jerry looked at him maliciously. "We don't fancy anything you recommend, Fatty."

"Anyway," added Harry, "what are you doing here,

besides growing fatter?"

Peter saw Brian flush with anger, so he stepped forward on his behalf.

"There was no need for that remark. It was a rotten thing to say."

"Oh, there was every need. He's a very fat boy. He needs someone to tell him. And he's also very nosy. Someone should tell him to mind his own business and stop asking questions about people. He might get hurt if he doesn't shut up."

Till that moment the sky had been fairly grey, but now the clouds broke and the sun suddenly shone through. As the yard brightened, Peter saw that Brian's bulky form was casting a substantial shadow on the asphalt. The other two were in the shadow of the doorway. If only he could get them to come forward …

"You're a rat," said Peter calmly, looking at Harry.

The other two looked at one another significantly.

"Calling us names is he, Jerry?"

"Yes, Harry," replied Jerry mockingly, "very bad names. We might have to do something about it, don't you think?"

To Peter, watching them carefully, they seemed so different from his old pals. These couldn't be the same Harry and Jerry who used to meet him in the gang hut. There was a darkness in their eyes that Peter had never seen before, and it made them look menacing.

"Come on," said Brian, "it's no use talking to them."

It was obvious that he could sense a fight coming, and he was nervous. He was afraid of pain, more than most people, and he had no wish to experience the agonies of a bloody nose or a broken tooth. He started to turn away, but Jerry was on his feet in a flash and moving towards him.

A well-aimed kick caught Brian hard on the ankles. The fat boy gasped with pain and hopped about on one leg. As he did so, Jerry kicked him on the other ankle.

At this, Peter stepped quickly across and hammered his fist straight into Jerry's left cheek. He felt the bone hard against his knuckles. This was no phantom, surely?

Suddenly, all the bitterness against the way he had been treated by these two welled up in him and he put Jerry flat on the ground with a murderous right cross. It was a sweet moment. Revenge.

"Look out, Pete!" warned Brian, failing to block Harry's headlong rush from the steps.

The force of the impact carried Peter to the ground and winded him. Before he knew what was happening, punches were landing about his head and neck.

Brian, fearful though he was, moved forward then, and with his eyes half shut whirled a fat fist in the general direction of the frenzied Harry. It caught him a glancing blow and distracted him long enough to enable Peter to squirm out from under his attacker.

Jerry was just struggling up when Peter planted another punch, right on the nose, and he collapsed in a heap once more. That just left Harry.

Backing away to give himself room, Peter told Brian to keep an eye on Jerry but otherwise not to interfere. Brian promptly went across and sat on Jerry's stomach. That one lucky blow had worked wonders for his confidence.

As their eyes met, Peter could see the hatred in Harry's dark gaze. They circled one another, then Harry rushed him. Peter was ready this time and side-stepped, sticking out a hard left into Harry's face as he overbalanced. Harry once again tried to get close, but once more Peter gave ground skilfully, scoring with two more blows at the last moment.

Harry glared at him, his chest heaving with temper, his fists tightly clenched. As he charged again, expecting Peter to give ground as before, his guard was down. Peter ducked slightly to the left, bobbed again and then hammered a left and right into Harry's solar plexus. His attacker was still gasping when Peter hit him on the side of the jaw.

Brian yelled with glee as he saw Harry tumble sideways on to the harsh surface of the playground. Forgetting about the threat posed by Jerry, he scrambled up and went over to Peter to pat him on the shoulder.

Jerry was on his feet immediately, a trickle of blood running from his nose, his face screwed into a tight scowl. In a second he had the plump boy down and was sitting astride him, punching him unmercifully.

With a shout, Peter lunged and barged him off. Jerry, blazing with anger, clutched at Peter and grappled with him, rolling him over on to the hard ground. The struggle was intense but brief, interrupted by a yell from Harry.

"Look out! Here's old Fishwick. Run!"

But it was too late.

"You boys there, Linton and Potter, and you other two, come here at once!"

The tall, thin master walked swiftly to meet them. The four dishevelled boys faced him somewhat apprehensively: he was noted for his strong views on the subject of fighting and he laid into them.

But Peter hardly heard a word. He was staring at the ground. There were five of them standing there in bright sunshine – but only three shadows.

CHAPTER 9

CAUGHT IN THE WEB

The cry, which had escaped Harry's lips as he was dropped into the well, still echoed in the black tunnel as if it belonged to somebody else. He could hear it ringing in his own ears as he plummeted down the shaft.

The descent seemed endless. The air whistled in his ears and dragged at his clothes, buffeting him all the way. Then, suddenly he was caught in a huge net. Soft as gossamer, but as strong as steel, it gave with the impact of his weight but did not break.

Before he knew what was happening, he was hauled in, dazed and battered, like a large fish. He was hoisted out of the shaft and into a small cave at the side of the tunnel. Torches flared all round him and he was aware of dim shapes moving on either side. Many hands were unravelling him from the soft web that held him. Someone was bending over him and calling his name again and again with great excitement.

"Harry! Harry! You're safe! You're with friends!"

It was Jerry.

Harry looked at the sea of faces crowded tightly around him. Eager hands steadied him as he tried to get to his feet.

"I don't understand," said Harry.

"Neither do I," replied Jerry. But it was clear from his smile that, here at least, they were in no further danger.

"You'll understand more about it in a little while," said a young man with fair hair worn long down to his collar. "My name's Alan. I found this place the same way as you did – via the well." He smiled. "It's quite a shock, isn't it?"

The boys introduced themselves to the young man and his companions and managed to shake most of the hands thrust out to them.

While they were talking, others were casting the net out into the shaft of the well and securing it to hooks driven into the wall.

"Come with us," said Alan. "Matthew must be informed of your arrival. He'll want to ask you some questions about the castle. Now, don't worry; you'll find him a wonderful old man. In fact, if it wasn't for him, none of us would have survived the fall into the well. Follow me."

They were led out into a long passage lit with torches thrust into niches in the walls. On their way they noticed that the passage divided every so often. Sometimes they went left and sometimes right. Eventually, they emerged into a large cave.

All around were beds of skins. The skins looked old and moth-eaten; there was hardly any fur on them. In the centre of the floor burned a fire near to which sat an old man with a head of white hair and a white beard; only his eyebrows retained a trace of their original darkness.

Alan introduced the two boys and they stood there a moment feeling strange and awkward.

"Harry and Jerry," repeated the old man, "I think I can

remember who is who." Smiling, he invited the boys to sit near the fire. "I'd like you to tell me – I should say *us* – your story from the beginning. How did you get here?"

There were now some forty or fifty people in the cave. Most of them were young, and most of them were men or boys, but there were four or five women and two teenage girls. The audience now assembled sat on the various beds about the fire. Their faces looked attentive, eager almost.

Harry took turns with Jerry to recount their adventures. No one interrupted.

When they had finished, Matthew said: "Well, as you can see, you are not the only ones to be tossed into the well. Look around. Sandra over there was the last to arrive before you. Before her came John and Mary Rodgers. They are all still a little confused and, as you no doubt are, a little depressed. They are wondering, like you, if they will ever escape from this place."

The old man stared at Harry and then Jerry, but there was a kindly gleam in his eye. "Believe me," he continued, "we all of us long for the day when we can return to our families and loved ones. Alas, I cannot say when that will be."

There was not a face in the company that did not look glum at the prospect of remaining trapped underground. One of the girls, Harry noticed, was weeping quietly. He felt on the verge of tears himself.

"I feel obliged to be honest with you," Matthew continued. "Nothing can be gained by giving you false hope. *But*," he said, emphasizing the word, "I can give you some real hope for the future. It is this: every time our little band grows in number, our potential for success increases.

With each new person arriving here, our resources are added to, positive action becomes more and more likely. Those of us who have been here the longest can feel a real gain in the strength of our resolution. Believe me, when I first came here, I was affected by a sort of all-pervading disablement, a sense of exhaustion that weighed upon my very limbs. Everything I did became an effort. Now, with the passing of time and the arrival of more people, I have felt that invisible load lightening. I am sure, if you think hard about it, the coming of Harry and Jerry just now can be felt by every one of us as a gain in our physical strength. Am I right?"

The assembled company looked at one another. One young man leapt up and flexed his arms, breathed deeply a few times, and shouted to the others near him: "Yes, it *is* true! I do feel stronger. I do seem to have more energy."

Matthew nodded. "That is our hope for the future. There is some special significance in this, if only we can recognize it. Once we have identified it, we can think how best to exploit it."

"In the meantime?" asked Alan.

"In the meantime," replied Matthew, "we continue our work of exploration. We have done much already."

"May I ask you a question, sir?" asked Jerry; and when Matthew nodded, he went on: "How did you come to be here?"

The old man seemed reluctant to relate his own story, knowing as he did that some of the company knew the outlines of it already; but the others pressed him to tell it again in more detail. So he began.

"Well, I was older than our two newcomers, of course –

twenty-three to be exact. I had always been interested in the world of the ancients, especially their religious and mystical beliefs. When I went up to Oxford I read Classics and I met a man in my college who was doing a research degree in Medieval History. He was writing a thesis on demonology in the Middle Ages. I thought him the most fascinating man I had ever met in my entire life. He had a commanding knowledge of his subject, and he was a wonderful speaker. I heard him give a lecture once to the Classical Society on the worship of the occult in Ancient Rome. He spoke with such authority that you could believe he had lived there in those very times he was speaking of. He had a wonderful voice, rich, hypnotic. When he began to talk, all other things faded from your mind; you were aware only of his voice, nothing else. When he stopped, it was like surfacing from great depths of ocean, an ocean of sleep. Uncanny!"

The old man seemed to shake himself free of the memory, and he looked at the boys.

"He used to invite me round to his rooms and we would talk late into the night, always about the occult, the power of Evil and its conflict with the forces of Good. One evening he told me he was working on an old Latin manuscript in the Bodleian Library. He was very excited about it because there was a description in the text of an ancient ritual supposed to have come down from Roman times. The detail, however, he kept to himself, saying that he had not completed his research yet. When it was finished, he said, he would ask me to help him with an experiment."

The old man gazed deep into the fire, stirring the

memories, as it were, as he shifted the embers about with the end of a stick he had taken up.

"What was his name, this man?" asked Alan.

Matthew smiled wanly. "Lucifer Magnus. That should have warned me about him, shouldn't it?"

"Lucifer – the fallen angel. Yes, I suppose it should," said Alan. "What about the manuscript he was working on?"

"Ah, that was written by a monk from Antwerp call Albinus. Magnus told me he had tried to trace him, but he had learned nothing about him apart for the fact the he had lived in Antwerp at the end of the thirteenth century and was reported to have perished rather horribly when a house he had been visiting was set on fire by an angry mob of townspeople."

"That is enough to whet anyone's appetite," said a man sitting near Alan. "Obviously this Albinus was unpopular."

Matthew nodded. "You can imagine how eagerly I waited for Magnus to finish his work. I did not see him all that week, for he was pressing on with his translation. However, I was to call on him in his rooms on the Saturday evening. I can remember quite vividly the thrill of excitement that ran through me when I saw that he had cleared the floor of his living-room and on it had drawn, in white chalk, a huge circle containing a five-pointed star. Here and there, there were strange symbols I had never set eyes on previously in anything I had read.

"It was obvious that Magnus was in a state of great excitement. His eyes were feverishly bright and the hollows in his cheeks were deeper than usual. Almost at once he began to jabber about the experiment. Albinus, he said, had discovered a method of projecting the spirit from the body and sending it elsewhere at will. The physical body would remain in a coma while the astral body was free to travel, visiting and observing whatever it wished. It could return, he told me, to the physical body whenever it desired.

"I was fascinated. Of course, I realized that the experiment could fail, but the thought that he might be lying never occurred to me. He was so very cunning, you see.

"The idea was, he said, that he should be his own guinea-pig. I was merely to be an observer. He had even provided a notebook for me to record events as they happened.

"My heart was thumping as I watched him fetch a candle from a cupboard and light it. He placed it in the centre of the circle and fixed it to the floor with a few drops of wax and then turned to fetch a book from his desk. As he crossed the line of the circle once more, he stumbled and cried out. I went to help him but he pushed me off, saying that he was all right. Almost immediately, however, he swayed on his feet and would have fallen if I had not supported him."

The old man shook his head at the memory.

"I didn't suspect a thing. I really thought he had sprained his ankle. I can hear him now, as if he were talking to me this minute. 'No,' he said, 'it's not my ankle. I just feel a little dizzy. I've been working too hard I suppose.' He said he'd have to postpone the experiment till he had recovered his health somewhat. It would be another month, though, before the moon was in the right phase again. He was sorry, he said, to disappoint me. You can imagine how I reacted to this!"

"I suppose you offered to take his place," observed Alan.

Matthew smiled ruefully. "No, Alan – I *begged* him to let me take his place. I said he could tell me what to do in stages."

The old man stared sadly into the firelight.

"He was a clever one, was Magnus. He put on a great show of wanting to be the first to try it; but I kept on at him – just as he knew I would. In the end he agreed.

"I helped him pull forward to the edge of the circle a large mirror on a stand. Till then it had been kept covered with a cloth. He uncovered it and began polishing it. When it was gleaming to his satisfaction, he draped the cloth round his shoulders and I can remember thinking it was like a black cloak.

"I stood where he told me, in the centre of the circle, and watched him take up the book from his desk. He began to read out, very slowly, the Latin incantation written there. As he read, I heard a sudden soughing of the wind in the eaves of the old house. A dull rumbling shook the chimney and the timbers seemed to groan beneath my feet. Suddenly, a bitter incense invaded my nostrils, and made my eyes water painfully. Fumes were filling the room with their acrid smoke and the candle at my feet flared up into a fountain of fire that was licking at my legs. I did not cry out, for I felt no pain from the flames; but as I watched, my feet seemed to melt away, and then my legs, and finally my whole body. I was so preoccupied with myself, that it was only at the last moment that I glanced at Magnus. It was then that I knew my danger, and that it was too late for me to save myself.

"He was shaking with silent laughter and mocking me with gestures and little bows and nods of the head. Beside him, at the edge of the circle, was the mirror. In it I caught sight of my reflection, or so I thought at first. But then I realized that the person in the depths of the glass, though he looked like me, had a life independent of mine; for he was walking towards the front of the mirror as if from a long way off, and it was not the interior of that room that I saw reflected there."

Matthew shook his head, as though trying to recall some elusive detail.

"It was as if I were looking into a large chamber. On all sides, in the gloom, there appeared to be sleeping forms draped in white. They did not move. Only this one shape coming towards the surface of the looking-glass had any life, and that life was apparently mine, for it bore my face.

"At that point I felt a great weight pressing down on my eyelids. When I opened them again, I was through the barrier, out of my own world."

Matthew's audience sat in awed silence for a moment. Then Jerry stirred.

"But how did you get here?" he asked.

"Much the same way as you did," the old man told him. "And here's a curious thing: you, and others before you, have always described Lucan and the young man in exactly the same way. It seems from what you say that neither of them has aged in any way. That fact may have some bearing on why we are here."

Alan spoke now. "As you might imagine, we have been here some time, and during that time we've had long discussions on the reason for our being here. The castle people make use of us in some way that we do not fully understand yet; but we're working to gain more knowledge. We feel certain that once we know why they have us here we shall then be much nearer to making our escape."

"Then there is some hope of getting back home?" asked Harry, beginning to cheer up a little.

"Yes, there is hope. There has to be hope. Without it we would die."

Harry's face lost its new-found cheer. There wasn't anything really definite after all, it seemed. He looked around: this cave was a bleak contrast to his home and all the little comforts he had taken for granted in the past.

"That net," said Jerry, prompting the old man to continue his story, "how did that get there?"

"Like you, I was dropped into the well by the giant, Lucan. I don't have to tell you what it was like plunging down into the blackness. Like you, I was caught in the net, or perhaps I should say web; for that is what it is. For several seconds I just lay there in the darkness, wondering what had happened. It was only when I saw green eyes glinting at me that I realized there might be some new danger. The only thing I possessed that might be any use as a weapon was a penknife. I was still fumbling for it when I saw something move towards me. There was a certain amount of light filtering down from the mouth of the well; for, unlike you, I arrived at the castle in the early morning, having spent the night perched uncomfortably in a tree."

"What was it?" demanded Jerry. "The thing that was

coming at you, I mean."

"A giant spider," said the old man. "About the size of a large dog."

Both boys shuddered, as did Matthew as he recalled the experience.

"I was terrified. The penknife seemed such a feeble thing to have to rely on. To make matters worse, when I struggled to sit upright, I found myself stuck fast, just as though I had fallen into a glue-pot. I could just about move my right arm. I often think that if my knife had been in my left trouser pocket I shouldn't be alive today. I could never have reached it in time.

"I felt the creature touch my foot as it came on to the web. Then it was astride my legs. I have never been so afraid in my life. Even the shock of falling into the well was not as bad.

"I could hear a sort of harsh whistling breathing coming from somewhere in its hairy body; and all the time its gleaming green eyes seemed to glare at me unwinkingly.

"I had the knife open. It was one of the spring-bladed knives; I used to use it for fishing trips. All it needed was a press of the thumb, thank God. Believe me, I did thank Him!

"I steeled myself for one desperate lunge. As its revolting body came within striking distance of my face, I slashed at it with the knife. I felt it writhe as I caught it with the blade; then suddenly it was gone and I was alone.

"I was still unable to raise myself properly, for the web was very sticky. All I could do was lie there and hope that the terrible creature would not come back. It took a long time for my nerves to calm down. Eventually I had a go at cutting myself free, but the strands were simply too tough. Perhaps it was just as well, for I could have spilled myself down into the darkness below."

"How did you get out of the web, then?" Jerry asked.

"After several hours the stickiness seemed to diminish and I was able to claw my way across to the small cave where you two boys were pulled to safety. There I found the body of the spider. I also found the remains of some of its victims."

Matthew's lips were set in a grim line as he paused for a moment. Then he went on:

"To my surprise, the web did not rot away, though it lost its stickiness Some months later another man fell into the net and I was able to help him into the cave."

"But what do you live on?" asked Harry. "What do you eat? Is there any food down here?"

Alan laughed and so did several of the others.

"Nobody eats food here You will never feel hungry, so you will never require anything to eat. Think about it. How long is it since you last had a meal?"

"Gosh," said Jerry. "I see what you mean The last thing I had was school dinner and it's hours and hours since then and I don't feel a bit hungry."

"But that's weird!" exclaimed Harry. "Why don't we feel hungry?"

"I am not certain, but it fits into the picture of things that we are beginning to build up," Matthew said thoughtfully.

"What about the man who came down here after you, the man you brought out of the web?" asked Harry.

"He was lost many years ago. We set out to explore the

labyrinth of caves that lead out from here and we got separated. He just seemed to vanish. One minute he was answering my calls, the next there was silence. I could find no trace of him."

"The caves are dangerous," observed Alan, "but we are learning our way about them. In the process, however, we seem to have lost one or two of our friends."

"What happened to them?" asked Harry, a touch of horror in his voice.

"We just don't know. Like Matthew's first companion down here, they simply seem to have vanished away."

"So there is no way out from here?" asked Jerry, disheartened.

"Well," admitted Alan slowly, "no one has managed to escape from here yet." He looked at Matthew as if inviting him to comment, but the old man remained silent.

Suddenly Harry had a thought: "Wherever do you get sticks for the fire? Surely no trees grow underground?"

Matthew turned his head and stared at him. After a moment's study of the boy, he said: "You're the first one, besides Alan, ever to notice the sticks. I think you and your friend are going to be very useful to us."

CHAPTER 10

AN UNEXPECTED ALLY

Peter and the others were all punished, but none of them would explain why they had been fighting, a fact which angered Mr Fishwick, who liked to think he knew everything that went on amongst the "natives", as he called the boys.

"Well, let that be a lesson to you," growled the master through his thin bitter lips. At six o'clock the boys stared at him gloomily, and trooped from the detention room when he nodded dismissal.

On their way up the road Brian said: "I meant to thank you for sticking up for me the way you did."

"Forget it," said Peter. "Those two had it coming to them. Listen, Brian, what I want to know is whether you'll come with me to Number Seven."

"Sure. I think the Magic Shop is at the bottom of this whole business, don't you?"

"That's what I aim to find out. Come on then."

Being the last week of term, Christmas was less than a fortnight off. Fairy-lights decorated many of the shop windows in a brave effort to combat the grim winter evening. They suggested warmth and cheerfulness, but the boys shivered in the biting east wind that was now sweeping along the street. Number Seven, of course, was in darkness.

"Creepy sort of place, isn't it?" muttered Brian, as if afraid of being overheard.

Peter said nothing but went straight to the window and looked in. There was nothing to see: no boxes, no packs of cards, no tricks, nothing. The shelves at the back of the window space were splintered. Beyond that he could see nothing in the gloom.

Brian tried the door. It was locked.

"It's closed down. They must have moved!"

It was odd how those words chilled Peter, who was still peering into the blackness at the back of the shop, searching eagerly for some trace of movement. But Brian was right – it was no longer the Magic Shop. All the same, there was still an evil feel to the place.

"It's weird," observed Brian.

Peter nodded.

"Listen, I was thinking we might slip round the back and take a look. There's a narrow entry at the rear."

The other boy nodded. "Right, let's go."

The lamp in the alley shone with a determined glare that cast deep shadows into corners and crannies. The wind lisped forlornly through the broken planks in the back gate of Number Seven. It was not locked.

"Got a torch?" asked Peter.

Brian had only a box of matches. Once inside, out of the wind, he struck a light and they saw that they were in a narrow paved yard. Several dustbins lined the wall on their right, all of them empty. One of them rocked slightly in a sudden fierce gust of wind and it rang with an eerie resonance. The match went out, but not before they glimpsed the only door into the building. Carefully they groped their way to it. To their surprise they found it unlocked.

"Wait," said Peter, heart thumping suddenly at the prospect of entering that deserted place. "Not so fast. Let's light another match."

In the instant before the match flared, Peter had a panic vision of that wrinkled old face peering at him through the dusty window-pane on that other evening after school. His chest tightened as he stood there watching the light growing from the head of the match and seeing the shadows stretch across the wall.

"Look," said Brian. He showed Peter a lump of wood with a nail in the end. "I found it down by the bins. I hope I don't have to use it."

They entered a narrow passage and, moving cautiously, reached the foot of a flight of bare wooden stairs. The match went out and blackness yawned at them. The only sound was the dull rumble of the wind round the walls outside.

"Come on," whispered Peter, "get another match lit. Quick!"

After much fumbling, Brian struck a third match and they moved towards the door at the end, the one leading them towards the front of the shop. With a creak like a coffin lid opening, the door swung back to reveal a long empty room. At the far end they could see the shop window illuminated by a lamp in the street outside. All around were empty shelves. On the right, near the door, was a counter.

Another match showed them just how bare the shop was now. The only thing on view was dust. The place might have been empty for years for all the sign of occupation there was now.

"Look what I've found!" called Brian, stooping.

"It's an erasor," said Peter, peering at it.

There were markings on it. "Look – J.P. Jerry Potter," said Brian. "So they *did* come in here. This proves it."

Peter nodded grimly. The thing was Jerry's all right. He'd borrowed it often enough to know it well.

"They both denied coming in here," he mused aloud. "Why should they lie about it? I can't see the point."

Before Brian could reply, there was a sudden rattle on the window, and the boys looked up to see the helmeted features of a policeman peering in.

The match was doused immediately and in less time than it takes to tell, they were in the yard and sprinting for the back gate. They burst through and only stopped running when they reached Park Road, which bounded Richmond Park, where the gang hut was. It seemed the obvious place to hide, so Peter took Brian to the gap in the railings and they squeezed through. Brian only just made it.

There was something about the appearance of the hut that told Peter it had not been used since the evening when Harry and Jerry had sat with him, talking of their proposed visit to Number Seven. Obviously, Harry and Jerry no longer visited the gang hut. Perhaps it was to avoid him.

The two boys talked over the day's events, speculating on the causes of Harry's and Jerry's lack of shadows, and wondering why the Magic Shop had closed down. Why, they asked each other, had Jerry Potter changed from a cheerful joking sort of boy into a mean and spiteful creature? Why had Harry taken to minor acts of bullying in remote corners of the playground?

They could not solve any of these puzzles, and when they left after about an hour, they were both touched by a sense of unease. Both felt inwardly that the Harry and Jerry they now saw every day in school were no longer the Harry and Jerry they used to know. In some mysterious way they had changed. Brian was obsessed by the concept of the *doppelgänger*, his head being full of the stories he had been reading. Peter could not quite bring himself to believe that, but he was nevertheless disturbed, and his natural sensitivity had been affected by the odd behaviour of his friends. There was plainly a great enigma centred in those two.

Strangely enough, it was the very next day that they found a source of help and advice – and in a most unexpected quarter.

Mr Carter, the English teacher, was away ill. In his place the class had a Mr Stokes, a teacher who had joined the school at half-term.

The lesson concerned creative writing and the chosen subject was *Fear*. One of the boys asked if he could write a ghost story and Mr Stokes said that it would be very appropriate. To illustrate, the teacher told them a story about a house in Norfolk where shadows whispered and doors creaked open unexpectedly. The master had a deep rich voice and he told his tale vividly with gestures and contortions of the face. Pongo Warton laughed at first, but he became strangely silent as the story unfolded. To cap it all, Mr Stokes informed them that it was a true story and that he himself had visited the house.

Then the boys settled down with a will. Time seemed to gallop along, and before anyone had finished, the bell was ringing for lunch.

"You can finish the story for homework tonight," said Mr Stokes, picking up his things. "Hand your books in to this boy here," he added, pointing at Peter. "You can call at the staffroom at morning break. Don't make me come and look for you."

Most of the class barged out of the room as soon as they were dismissed, but Peter and Brian lingered.

Just as Mr Stokes picked up his bag, Brian said: "Excuse me, sir. Do you know a lot about ghosts and that sort of thing?"

Mr Stokes turned and looked at him. He was one of those men who, at first glance, look younger than they really are. A closer, longer look revealed a network of fine lines round the eyes and the corners of the mouth. His fair hair, too, had touches of silver at the temples.

He replied: "Well, it is a hobby of mine. I like to think that I know more than most about the supernatural. Not just ghosts."

"I was wondering …" faltered Brian.

"Yes?"

Brian suddenly blurted out his interest in *doppelgängers*, and told the master about the story he had been reading.

"Do you think they really exist, sir? Or are they just

something in a story?"

Mr Stokes looked at him seriously. It was impossible to tell from his expression what he was thinking.

After a long pause, he said: "I have heard that instances of *doppelgänger* manifestation are on record in Bavaria dating from the nineteenth century. And the *doppelgänger* features in German folklore generally."

"There are two of them in this school, sir!"

Mr Stokes stared at Brian, unsmiling, stern even.

"It's true, sir," insisted Brian, anxious to be believed

Mr Stokes put down his bag and sat on the edge of a desk. He looked first at Brian's earnest face, then at Peter. When he spoke, his voice was quiet and serious. "I don't really think this is a good idea for a joke, do you?"

"It *isn't* a joke, sir," insisted Peter, watching the master's face for signs of growing irritation.

"Either you are a pair of very good liars, or you are mistaken."

"We're not lying, sir."

"Then you are mistaken," he said firmly and rose to leave.

"Please, sir," said Brian, "we've *got* to tell someone. We need help!"

Mr Stokes hesitated. At last he said: "What makes you so sure we have *doppelgängers* here?"

Between them, the boys told him about Harry and Jerry and the Magic Shop and all the things that had happened. It was well into the lunch-hour before they finished.

"You say this shop is empty now?"

"Yes. And it looks as if it has been empty for years."

There was a pause.

"I'll tell you what I'll do. I'll look into this business of the shadows, and then, if I find you have been telling the truth, I'll prepare a mirror test."

He looked at the signs of relief on the boys' faces and realized how deadly serious they were.

"Have you told anyone else about this?" he asked.

They shook their heads.

"Well, don't." He went on grimly: "You must keep it to yourselves for the time being. Not a word to anyone. And I mean, *anyone* – your parents included!"

CHAPTER 11

LIFE UNDERGROUND

It was difficult for the boys to measure the passing of time in the caves because there was no daylight. They had to rely on others telling them when it was time to go to bed. Even so, it was difficult to sleep. The small community kept watch all the time, posting guards at various key points, so people were coming and going in the main living-chamber at regular intervals.

From time to time Harry and Jerry visited the shaft of the well and peered upwards at the tiny circle of light that was the mouth of the well. However, after a while, they found it a rather depressing experience, so they kept to the caves, trying to occupy themselves with the small daily tasks allocated to them.

Naturally, they were both terribly homesick. They were also worried about the anguish their disappearance would be causing their parents and friends.

"You're bound to feel homesick," said Matthew, one day soon after their arrival, noticing how unhappy they looked. "The answer is to keep busy. Every day Alan or I give out a list of jobs to be done. Some of them may not seem very important, but I want you to carry out all your tasks conscientiously and to report anything unusual you may discover. You see, we are trying to build up a picture of the world we are now a part of. The more we know about it, the more likely we are to be able to cope with it. We must be as familiar with our territory as a hunter has to be with that of his quarry if he is to outwit it." He smiled sadly and added: "Not that I am a hunter by nature, you understand. I have never liked killing anything – even that spider I told you about."

Just then a girl of about fourteen wandered in; trailing behind her rather tearfully was her four-year-old brother.

Matthew called to her: "Ann, come and talk to us."

She came shyly towards them, her hand gently touching her young brother's shoulder to bring him along with her. She sat next to Matthew and pulled her dark fringe out of her eyes with her long, brown fingers. Still she didn't speak.

"I was just telling Harry and Jerry how to deal with that homesick feeling we all suffer from now and again. Ann came about ten days before you did. I thought it might interest the boys, Ann, if you were to tell them your story. It might prevent them feeling too sorry for themselves if they heard what happened to you and little Timmy."

Ann smiled slightly. It was obvious that she was making an effort to be cheerful for the sake of her little brother.

"Yes, please tell us," said Jerry. "You heard our story the other night."

The girl sighed and fingered her fringe once more in a

nervous sort of gesture.

"Well, it's hard to explain really. You see, I was playing a game with Timmy. I had been reading him a story about the Wicked Witch of the West – I think it was called *The Wizard of Oz*. Anyway, he wanted to play a game about spells and magic. He was going to change me into a frog or something." She looked shyly at her audience. "Not really, of course, just pretending. Anyway, there was knock on the door and it was old Mrs Gooding calling to see my mother.

"Well, Mum was out. We were on our own in the house. Mrs Gooding asked if she could come in and wait, and I said she could. She watched us playing for a while and then asked if she could join in. Timmy thought it would be great fun, because she did look more the part of the witch than I did. I mean, witches are supposed to be old, aren't they?"

"They are in all the books I've ever read," smiled Matthew.

"What happened then?" asked Harry.

"As I said, she joined in. Timmy was very pleased. He's only four and he loves games; and Mrs Gooding really entered into the spirit of it. I thought what a good sport she was."

Ann paused and it was plain that she was struggling to keep her tears in check. Matthew put his arm round her to comfort her.

"Perhaps you'd rather not tell us about it just now," suggested Harry, trying to be helpful.

The girl shook her head and brushed her tears away.

"She really fooled me. If *only* I'd known what sort of a

person she was. She should have been called Badding, not Gooding!"

"What did she do to you?"

"She said she was going to cast a spell on us and began to draw a large chalk circle on the kitchen floor."

"Where did she get the chalk from?" asked Matthew.

"Yes," said Jerry, "it's hardly the sort of thing the average old lady carries round with her, is it?"

"She had it in her handbag. I didn't really think about it at the time. Timmy was so excited that he could hardly wait for her to finish scribbling her wobbly shapes round the edge of the circle. Then she drew a huge star and put us in the centre. All the time, Timmy was squeaking: 'Make some spells, Mrs Witch! Make some spells!' Well, she did," said Ann grimly. "The next thing I knew was that I was standing outside the gates of a huge castle and Timmy was screaming his head off. The rest you can guess."

"An old lady?" asked Harry. "She did that to you and your little brother?"

"And you knew her?" added Jerry.

"Yes. She's lived in the house at the end of the street for over thirty years. I never liked her very much, but I never thought ..." Ann's words trailed off helplessly.

"There you are," observed Matthew quietly. "It shows you that there are many people involved in this business, sometimes people you would never suspect. Their object seems to be to secure a constant supply of prisoners, though for what reason I am not sure. For one thing, not everyone is dropped into the well. Most are taken into the Great Hall, but what happens there I have no idea. You see, there are some people here with us who, like Ann, came through the barrier with a companion. The companion was dragged away to the Great Hall, or the Keep in some instances, while they were hurled into the well. It is, I am afraid, still a great puzzle."

Just then, Alan arrived. It was obvious that he had something to tell Matthew, but he glanced at the others, as though uncertain whether to speak in front of them.

"Is it going well?" asked Matthew, somewhat cryptically. "You have had some success?"

Alan nodded.

"Good. Then we'll call a meeting. I'd like everyone here in the living-chamber."

Half an hour later the entire company was assembled, some of them having walked a considerable distance it appeared, judging by the stray remarks Harry overheard. It seemed to him, looking about him at faces he had not seen before, that there was still a great deal he did not understand about this underground world.

Matthew and Alan, and a tall man the boys had not seen before, counted heads. Satisfied that no one was missing, Matthew began to address the meeting.

"Friends, I have something important to announce. Joshua, here, has been working for some time now at the far end of the upper level. His gallery, as some of you know, runs directly under the castle dungeons. Fifteen days ago he discovered a door at the end of what he had previously thought was simply a fissure in the rock wall."

There were cries of excitement from all sides, and Matthew had to hold up his arms for silence before he could continue.

"I can tell by your excitement that you understand the implications of this discovery."

"But fifteen days ago, you said," called a woman with greying hair. She was clasping the hand of her meek-looking husband. "Why haven't you spoken of this before now?"

"Because we had to make sure that the door could be opened without exposing us to the attention of the castle people. We all know what it is like to be on the receiving end of their interest."

Joshua now spoke up. "It would have been foolish to think that all we had to do was open the door and walk to freedom. The one thing that we surely must have learned by now is that this world we are trapped in is full of surprises, most of them unpleasant. So, we were determined not to lose any advantage that we might have gained. Alan, George and Les each examined the door minutely. We also listened carefully for several hours for sounds of movements on the far side. Only when we were satisfied that it was reasonably safe to proceed did we try to force the door open. If you have ever tried to force a door that opens towards you, you'll know how difficult it was for us to get that door open!"

Again voices rose in chattering excitement. So the door was open! They could pass through? It was a good two or three minutes before the babble died down.

At last Joshua was able to continue. "We have been in the castle."

There was more noise, more shouting.

"Yes, we have explored, and returned safely. That is the important thing."

It took Matthew some time to restore order to the meeting. He held up his arms and spread them wide till every voice fell silent.

"We must be quite certain of one thing." He was speaking very slowly and with measured pauses to emphasize his words and drive them home. "We may have but one hope, one chance of escape. Therefore, we must weigh our actions very carefully before we make any move. One mistake," and here he scanned the faces around him, "one mistake might seal our fate for ever."

His keen eyes searched their watchful expressions for any sign of foolhardy impatience.

"Every man, woman and child in this chamber wants passionately to escape. No one knows better than I do the longing to be home, the desire for one's family, friends, fireside. But it is precisely now that we must ask ourselves what we mean by 'escape'. What shall we achieve by simply rushing out through that door? Where shall we escape to?"

Again he stared about him, looking into their eyes as if he sought to look into their very souls.

"For me, escape means getting back to my own world. It means fleeing this cave network, fleeing the castle, fleeing the terrible people who inhabit those lofty halls and grim battlements. That is the escape that I am looking for; and that, I am sure, is the escape you desire, too."

"Matthew is right," said Alan. "That door is only the beginning. For the first time ever we may have an advantage. We mustn't waste it. Joshua, Matthew and I all feel that if there is a way for us to be brought through the barrier in one direction – and we know that there is, because we are here – then there must be a way for us to go back. It was the castle people who transported us into this world of theirs, so it would seem most likely that they are the ones who possess the knowledge we need to enable us to return."

"But how are we going to gain that knowledge from them? It's impossible. They'd never tell us." It was Mrs Grey- hair again.

"You are quite right," agreed Alan. "They would never tell us, not consciously, not willingly. But we might discover the secret from them without their knowing they had told us a thing."

There were cried of: "Impossible! Don't talk rubbish!"

Joshua stepped forward again. "I'll tell you how, if you will listen to me. The door enters the castle via a secret tunnel. Alan and I have already explored some of it, and there appears to be a network of secret passages running inside the walls. Here and there you can look into a chamber, even the Great Hall. We've watched the castle people, and it is my opinion that we can learn by observing them. We must prepare our plans carefully and only reveal our hand when we're in a strong position to act. Matthew is our leader, and the wisest of us all. He will guide us well, as he has guided us in the past. We must all, without exception, agree to be bound by his decision. Do you agree?"

There was a general murmur of assent throughout the cave as Matthew stepped forward to address them once more.

"We shall split up into groups," he announced. "Each party of ten will have a leader. That leader will take his orders from Alan, Joshua, George and Les. I propose we mount a round-the-clock watch on the castle people. There will be some of us in the secret passages, watching and listening, throughout the day and night. Our aim is to find out all we can about these people. Remember, our watchword will be 'knowledge is strength'; every bit of information gained is a weapon to our hand."

Harry looked at Jerry. For the first time since their arrival there was a gleam of hope in his eyes.

CHAPTER 12

THE MIRROR TEST

"I must apologize to you," said Mr Stokes two days after the boys had told him about Jerry and Harry. "I thought you were pulling my leg; but now I have seen for myself. You're right. There *is* something wrong here. But, if I'm going to help, I need to know everything I can about the background. Now, tell me about the Magic Shop again."

They told him everything they knew, even about the visit to the premises and the headlong flight from the policeman. Mr Stokes listened in silence, nodding from time to time.

When they had finished, he said: "I have a good idea how the *doppelgänger* can be created, but what really concerns me is *why*. Why should anyone do this to a couple of schoolboys? I can't see the reason for it at all."

He stared thoughtfully at the ground for a while, and then went on: "I wonder ... I suppose it might be worth a try; at least it's better than doing nothing." He turned to the boys. "The Central Reference Library may give me the clue. Look, meet me by my car after school. We'll pop into town and see what we can find out."

Eagerly the boys agreed, and at half-past four they were

pushing through the doors into the warmth of the Reference Library.

Without hesitation, Mr Stokes walked over to the banks of catalogues and began to pull out several of the thick, squat volumes. As he flicked over the pages, he jotted down titles, and, ten minutes later he was seated, watched by the boys, at a large reading table, poring over a selection of old, musty books bound in leather.

They browsed in silence for about an hour until Mr Stokes gave a grunt of satisfaction.

"I think I have it. I'll just take a few more notes, then I'll explain it to you."

It was six o'clock when they left the library. Mr Stokes offered to drive the boys back to school where he had to pick up some books of his own from the staff-room.

As he drove through the traffic, he explained what he had read about. "In the days of the Roman Empire, and later in Medieval Germany, it was believed that life could be prolonged by capturing the souls of others and using them as a source of energy for oneself. These souls were thought to be transported to a sort of other-world, a shadow-kingdom which touches ours at a tangent, suspended in time, invisible to the human eye, but accessible."

"Is it true?" asked Peter uneasily.

Mr Stokes laughed. "Well, who can say? No one has thought so for centuries. And yet," he added, as though reluctant to admit it, "it seems as if there is someone who knows all about it; that is, if Potter and Sellers are what we think they might be."

"But the *doppelgänger*, sir, how does that fit in?"

"You're asking a great deal of me, Linton. Like you, I'm feeling my way in this business. All I know is that in German folklore the *doppelgänger* is taken as a sign of death – if you see your own *doppelgänger*, that is. But here we seem to have something different. A person's likeness, or mirror image, is taken and used as a means of living here in *our* world.

"As you know, the ancients always regarded mirrors and reflections with something approaching awe. It is only we, living in the modern world, who take it all for granted without bothering to think about it very carefully."

They reached the school and Mr Stokes pulled into the car park and switched off the engine. Just before he opened the door, he said: "Think about a mirror for a moment. When you look into a glass and see the room reflected there, you're gazing into a world of reversals. Supposing you were to open the door that you see reflected there, the one in the mirror I mean, what then? How can you know what is on the other side of that door? While you look into the mirror, you think you can see the familiar surroundings of your home, but even that image is a lie, really. You raise your right hand: the person staring out at you raises his left. The thoughts that are running through your head – are the same thoughts running round in his? Can you ever hope to know the schemes in his mind? Do you see what I'm driving at?"

Peter nodded.

"I never thought of people in mirrors having thoughts," observed Brian.

"None of us would. To us, this world of the mirror is

alien, but the ancients respected what they failed to understand. They kept an open mind. In our day and age we reject what doesn't fit in with our scientific theories. We're too arrogant to admit that our theories are incomplete. Instead, we pride ourselves on knowing it all."

Mr Stokes looked from one to the other of them before going on: "Well, we may have stumbled on something that the ancients in their humble ignorance knew about but which we, in our modern pride of learning, know nothing of. There's a paradox for you."

"Do you think," asked Brian hesitantly, "that someone is using Harry's or Jerry's mirror image to be able to live in our world?"

"Well, it is a thought," replied Mr Stokes, shrugging.

"But why Harry? Why Jerry? What's so special about them?"

"They are both young. They have all their lives ahead of them. Who wants to take over an old man's life? Besides, the young are easier to trap. They are, you must forgive my saying, more gullible."

"Gosh, yes! That's it! Harry and Jerry went to the Magic Shop and were trapped by the old man. Do you think he could be the one using them?"

"What shall we do about it, sir?" asked Brian.

"What *can* we do?" observed Peter gloomily.

"Well, for a start, we must arrange a mirror test for Sellers and his friend," said the master. "You will have to help me with that …"

The following day Harry Sellers and Jerry Potter were sent for, one at a time, by Mr Stokes. He was sitting at his desk. Opposite him, propped up against the front of a pupil's desk, was a mirror concealed by a heavy cloth. Peter was standing in front of the mirror. When the mirror was uncovered, Mr Stokes was able to see a fine reflection of himself from where he sat. Anyone standing immediately in front of his desk would also be clearly visible in the mirror. At a signal from him, Peter was to stand aside and uncover the mirror. In this manner it was hoped that the test would be conducted without Harry or Jerry being any the wiser. As a bit of extra camouflage, several other boys were also to be summoned for interview.

Jerry's turn came to enter the room.

"Ah, there you are, Potter. Come over here. I've got something to say to you."

"Sir?"

"Last Tuesday I set you an essay for homework. Would you mind telling my why you didn't do it?"

Jerry blinked. "It was a story, sir. We did a bit of it in class and you told us to finish it off for homework."

"I'm well aware of that. I asked you where it was."

"But you said it was an essay, sir. I didn't write an essay. I wrote a story."

"A story, then! But where is it?"

"Linton has it, sir."

"But he assures me he hasn't."

"I gave it to him on Wednesday morning."

"You're quite sure?"

"Yes, sir."

"Humph," snorted Mr Stokes, feigning puzzlement. "Then it must have been mislaid. I'll have another look for it in the staffroom. You may go."

When they were alone, Peter asked the master about the image.

"There was no reflection, Linton. The only person I saw was myself. All the other boys had reflections in the glass, but not Potter. Now," he went on grimly, "let's see what friend Sellers looks like."

The result was the same.

After school the boys met Mr Stokes in the car park.

"What next, sir?"

"You'd better come round to my flat this evening. I've been reading up on the subject, and I think I have a plan for dealing with this situation."

"What is it, sir? Can we get Harry and Jerry back, do you think?"

But Mr Stokes refused to go into detail.

All he said was: "Be at my flat at eight o'clock. Here's the address."

CHAPTER 13

THE DUNGEONS

"We've made an important discovery," said Alan, looking serious.

He was about to lead Harry and Jerry into the passageway beneath the castle. It was to be the boys' first venture through the wooden door at the top of the steps.

"We've found another group of prisoners."

"People like us?" gasped Harry.

Alan nodded. "We haven't done anything about releasing them yet. We had to wait till Matthew had been informed. Well, now he has, and after discussing it with Joshua and me and the other group leaders, he's come to a decision. We are going to free them."

"Gosh! And you're taking us with you?"

"Yes. It is your turn to come with me. The main party has gone ahead on its normal exploration of the passages. They'll be reporting back to Matthew direct this time. The three of us will have a closer look at the cells where the other prisoners are locked up."

"What about the guards?" asked Harry. "Can we get past them?"

"That's the odd thing," said Alan. "There don't appear to be any guards down there. We know there are people moving around, because we've seen them in other parts of the castle, but in the dungeons there appear to be only prisoners. There must be a reason for that, but we don't yet know what it is."

Alan now showed them some pointed metal rods he was carrying.

"We found these in the passages yesterday," he said. "They'll come in handy for forcing the doors of the cells. Here, you can carry one each. Carefully! They're not exactly light, as you can see."

Harry took his long metal rod and laid it on his shoulder, the spike pointing upwards. Meanwhile, Alan led the way carrying their only torch.

After about forty yards, Harry stopped.

"What's the matter?" asked Alan.

"It's my legs," said Harry. "They're aching. I feel as if I've just run a mile at top speed."

"Me, too." agreed Jerry, glad to stop.

"I should have warned you," said Alan. "Joshua thinks it's the influence of the castle. This time it's much worse than before."

They set off once more, but fairly soon they had to stop again to let Harry rub his leg muscles in an effort to massage some relief into them. Jerry copied him.

Alan looked grim. "This is something I didn't bargain for. It really is very difficult to make progress. I can't understand it."

"Do you know what it's like?" ventured Harry. "It's like trying to run when you're having a nightmare. You know, when you're being chased by something horrible and you're trying to escape, but your legs just don't seem to work somehow."

Alan nodded thoughtfully. "You're absolutely right. It's just like that. We're being held back by some force down here. But why haven't I felt it as severely as this before? I've been in these passages several times already and not felt this effect."

He rose from where he had been crouching, took a step forward and then stopped.

"What's that?" asked Jerry. "I can hear something!"

Round a bend ahead came the wavering light of a torch. Shortly after, the first of the returning exploration party appeared.

"What are you doing back here so soon?" asked Alan, sounding annoyed.

"We can't go on, Alan. The going's too heavy. I've never felt so weary in my life," replied the leader, a man called Adam. The others behind him in the passage nodded.

"So you're giving up?"

"Look, don't be angry, Alan. We think Matthew should be told, because this is something new. None of us has ever felt this effect before in the passages, so it could be important."

"I'm sorry," said Alan. "You're right. We ought to report back. Come on, we'll go together."

Matthew listened to them in silence.

When they had finished, he said: "How many in the exploration party?"

"Six."

"How many normally?"

"Ten. Why do you ask?"

"Alan, when you went into the passages that first time with Joshua, did you feel anything like this then?"

Alan looked puzzled. "Well … I suppose I did, but I had been working for ages with Joshua trying to get that door open, and we were in a very cramped position most of the time. Naturally, my legs felt very weary, but I didn't think much about it. Besides, we didn't go very far the first time."

Matthew nodded. "And the next time you went into the passages, how many of you were there?"

Alan thought for a moment. "About a dozen, I suppose."

"Any unusual effects then?"

"No, not that I was aware of. But what's so important about the numbers involved?"

"It is just a theory I have."

"I think I know what you are hinting at," said Harry excitedly. "I remember something you said to us not long after Jerry and I came underground."

Matthew smiled, waiting to see if the boy was right.

"You said that every time someone joined the community you felt stronger. Each new member of the group brings strength, a strength which we all experience. You said, Matthew, that when you were first down here you and your companions always felt exhausted."

Matthew nodded, pleased that Harry had worked it out for himself.

"I see what you mean," said Alan, leaning forward eagerly. "It *is* something to do with numbers. There's too few of us to combat the force that weighs us down in the passages."

"The point you must take note of," said Matthew, "is that you are now entering the castle. It is only to be expected that you will be subject to its power, its influence. The only way to fight against that power is to move about in sufficient numbers, keeping close together, and doing what you have to do together. If you split up, you will be weakened. It is only your combined strength that can counter the energy field of the castle."

"Was it like that when you were alone at the bottom of the well?" asked Jerry.

"Yes. Just like that. You see, the castle's power extends a great distance beyond its courtyard, its corridors and its turrets. It must be surrounded in all directions by an energy field. It is like being caught in a powerful magnetic force."

"Right," said Alan, "we shall have to revise our plans. Instead of just three of us going to the cells, we'll need at least ten. It would be safer if there were only three of us – less chance of being seen. But if ten of us are needed to get through, then ten of us will have to go. We'll just have to be that much more careful."

"But you said there were no guards to worry about in the dungeons," reminded Jerry.

"I said there didn't *appear* to be any. That's not quite the same," replied Alan.

"Be careful," warned Matthew. "You mustn't take a thing like that for granted. Be on your guard constantly."

After resting for about an hour to recover their strength, a group of ten, led by Alan, set off back to the passages. It was not long before Alan was tugging at an iron ring set in the rock wall. To everyone's surprise, the ring yielded to his hand and moved forward about two inches. Immediately a dull rumble warned the group that some hidden mechanism had been tripped. Moments later a gap in the wall opened up and they cautiously stepped through.

"Well," whispered Harry to Jerry, who was walking beside him at the rear of the group, "Matthew was right about the force lessening when you have sufficient numbers. I haven't got any pains in my legs and arms now."

"Keep quiet at the back," hissed someone.

It was not far to the cells, and up till now there had been no sign of guards. They approached the first door and gathered round to examine it, wondering how best to set about freeing the prisoner inside.

It was a solid, heavy door of rough timber studded with iron, with a large keyhole on the left side. There was no grating or window through which they could look.

"Who's there, outside?" croaked a man's voice.

"Friends," whispered Alan urgently. "We've come to help you."

At that, to everyone's astonishment, the cell door opened inwards and a small but stocky man in his mid-fifties stood blinking in the torchlight.

"But the door's not locked!" exclaimed a boy called Max. "Why is that?"

"I opened it years ago, centuries, eons since. Well, I'm exaggerating, of course, but it was a long time ago."

"We came to rescue you," said Alan, nonplussed by the man's matter-of-fact attitude.

The man laughed. "You're wasting your time. Look!" He swept his arm to his right to indicate the row of cell doors beyond his own. "There are nine other cells in this block and not one is locked. We've managed to get them all open, yet what do we find when we get out into the corridor? There's nowhere to go to."

He stared curiously round at them all.

"I suppose you've escaped from one of the other galleries," he observed. "Listen, take my advice. Go back where you came from. It isn't worth the drain on your energy."

Alan tried to interrupt him, but the man carried on, speaking earnestly.

"I know what I'm talking about. Believe me, it's not worth the agony of dragging yourself along these passages. It's like walking in deep water down here. It's impossible to get any speed up at all. Even if you could get out through the iron doors upstairs you'd never have the strength to fight off the guards. You'd be flattened and thrown back in your cell. You'd have wasted your effort."

Suddenly another cell door opened and then another.

A voice called: "What's going on, Ivor?"

"We've got some brave heroes here come to rescue us. Good joke, eh?"

It must have been, for they all laughed at Alan's party.

Alan himself looked distinctly upset. He beckoned to the others to join him. "Can you get everyone out of the cells? I've got something to say to you."

The man called Ivor shrugged and then shouted at the top of his voice: "Meeting, everyone! Assembly time.

Come on, get off your beds!" He did not seem to be taking the matter very seriously.

People emerged from the dark, rubbing their eyes in the unaccustomed torchlight. They were all, without exception, dressed entirely in scruffy rags, their faces grimy, their hair long and matted. And they stank.

"There's no water for washing down here," said Ivor, somewhat defensively. "I don't know how you lot manage to keep clean. Have you a hot water supply in your block?"

Other questions came from the cell-dwellers and their voices swelled to a torrent of sound in the stone passageway. Alan, fearful of the attention of guards, tried to hush them, but Ivor merely laughed.

"They won't bother to come down here. They know we're powerless." He laughed again. "Besides, I don't think they relish the smell of us."

The others laughed, too. They weren't in the slightest bit self-conscious about their appearance or condition.

"There's something strange about this lot," muttered Harry in Jerry's ear. "I'm not sure I like them very much."

"They've got a funny attitude all right," agreed Jerry. "I think we should get back to the secret door and leave them to it."

Harry said: "We'll have to see what Alan decides. He's the leader."

Ivor, who seemed to be the spokesman for his group, was still talking. "We're really quite happy here, you know. Our cells aren't half as bad as you think. Take a look for yourselves."

He stepped back into his own cell, and Alan followed with some of the others from his party, including Harry and Jerry.

"Look at that!" gasped Harry, pointing to the wall on his left. "What is it?"

Ivor was chuckling with satisfaction as his visitors stared, stupefied, at the dim scene being enacted for them on the wall of the cell.

"You've got a television in here!"

"No," said Ivor, with something akin to glee in his voice.. "Not television."

"It's a film, then!" said Jerry, "It must be."

"Wrong again!" tittered Ivor.

"But it's a moving picture of some sort. How does it ... where does it come from?" asked Alan.

Ivor threw himself down on his bed, his tousled head on the straw pillow. In the half-light from the torches in the passage outside, a smile could be seen settling over his broad features. He looked smugly at Alan. "You know, it's not half bad here, not bad at all."

"But the pictures," said Alan, trying to bring Ivor back to the topic under discussion. "Where do they come from? Is this some form of device?"

"I suppose," said Ivor slowly, half abstracted, his gaze still on the moving pictures unravelling themselves on the wall, "I suppose they're ..."

His voice trailed off and Alan had to prod him to get him to continue.

"I suppose it's magic. After all, we got here by magic, didn't we?"

"Hey!" whispered Harry, digging an elbow into Jerry to

get his attention. "The pictures seem sort of funny, don't they? I mean they're more like moving patterns. You look at them, and you think at first they're the same all the time, like a pattern being repeated over and over again. But they're not. When you watch the colours carefully, you can see things taking shape, growing extra bits."

"Extra bits?"

"Yes – look. I can see a tree there in the middle ... and now it's growing branches in all directions, and leaves. Wherever you look there are leaves forming ... Can't you see?"

"It doesn't look like a tree to me," said Jerry, his voice a little leaden. "I can see ants ... thousands of ants, all moving in a vast heap, crawling over one another all the time. Everywhere I look I see ants ..."

Suddenly Harry was being pulled out of the cell. He could feel someone shaking him by the shoulders, and hear a voice that seemed to be coming from far away. It took some moments before he realized that it was Alan, shouting at him.

"We've got to get away from here!" Alan was saying urgently.

The group from the caves was gathered round him in the passage. The cell people had all returned to their separate cells and shut the doors after them.

"What's the matter with those people?" asked Max, the tall youth with fair hair. "Don't they want to escape?"

"They're hypnotized or something, by the look of them," said Alan, "Under a spell of some kind which makes them like it here."

"Yes," observed a rather shaken Harry, "those pictures

107

were fascinating. I couldn't help watching them. I felt that something was about to happen at any moment, and if only I could carry on watching I would see something really exciting."

"Come on," said Alan firmly. "We're going back to Matthew. He has got to be told about this."

"Shouldn't we try to persuade those people to come back with us?" asked Max.

When Alan spoke, his face was grim. "I think we should go back right away. We must leave this place and these people. There's nothing but evil here!"

"But surely we must *try* to rescue them," urged Max. "We can't just leave them here!"

Alan paused, looking thoughtfully from one to the other of his followers. Suddenly he moved back towards Ivor's cell. "All right, lend a hand. Get the others out of their cells." And he flung open the door of Ivor's cell. Harry was close behind him when he entered.

"Come with us, Ivor. This place is evil. You must make an effort."

But this time Ivor took no notice of the interruption; he continued to smile stupidly at the wall with its moving pictures.

Alan stepped closer and prodded him. "Come on. It's for your own good."

He didn't even get a reply. Whatever novelty value the visitors might have had at first had now entirely evaporated.

Alan glanced at Harry and muttered grimly: "We must do something to get him up off that bunk and out of here. Give me a hand with him."

But as soon as they touched him, Ivor reacted savagely. Whirling ferociously upon them with his bony fists, snarling his foul breath into their faces and yelling a string of obscenities, he drove them out of his cell and slammed the door behind them.

The others along the passage fared no better. One of the party was clutching a gash on his cheek as he rolled out into the corridor. Each door was now firmly barred to them. They were not wanted, and the help that they had come to offer had been firmly rejected.

Disconsolate, they retraced their steps up the passage to the opening in the wall from which they had emerged. They arrived just in time to see it rumbling shut.

CHAPTER 14

THE FACE OF THE ENEMY

Peter never could explain just why he thought of going to see the vicar. Admittedly, St Andrew's was the local parish church, but Peter's family were not particularly regular church-goers, and Peter had never previously said any more than "Good morning" to Mr Grant. It was somewhat strange, then, that Peter should now be standing on the doorstep of the vicarage, waiting for the door to open.

It was an old house, set it its own grounds, which had seen better days. The white stucco was peeling from the walls at the front of the house. The paint on the woodwork round the windows was old and cracking. The trees that bounded the neglected lawn were tall and straggling and bare of leaves.

A cold wind was blowing and Peter stamped his feet to keep them warm and to keep his spirits up; for the night seemed to crowd close upon him and the shifting of the trees in the darkness unnerved him.

A light went on in the hall, then footsteps echoed, and eventually, with a rattle of chains, the wide heavy door was opened. A middle-aged woman blinked out at him over the top of her glasses.

"Yes?" she inquired in a pleasant voice, "have you come about the carol service on Sunday?"

"No," hesitated Peter, "I need to see the vicar on another matter ... if it's convenient."

"Oh. Have you an appointment? I mean, is my husband expecting you?"

"No, I'm afraid not."

"Oh, dear. He's so busy with the preparations for the Christmas services that I doubt ..." Her voice trailed off at the sight of Peter's obvious disappointment. She opened the door a little wider. "Is it an urgent matter?"

Peter nodded.

She looked at him doubtfully for a moment and then, stepping aside, beckoned him in. "Wait here, and I'll go and have a word with him. He's in the study."

Peter found himself in a stone-flagged hall. On the walls were some coloured prints of old London.

"Come this way," called Mrs Grant, leading Peter along the passage to the rear of the house.

Ahead of them a face popped out of a doorway and a voice said: "Come into the study, young man. Mary, dear, some tea perhaps?"

The vicar's wife trotted off to the kitchen while Peter was shown into the room and ushered into a comfortable, if worn-looking, wing chair facing the vicar's huge Victorian desk.

Mr Grant, like his wife, was middle-aged. He was a tall man with greying hair and vigorous eye-brows. His eyes, which were blue, were cheerful and his voice was crisp, but friendly.

"Well, what can I do for you? Not getting married, are

you?"

"No." said Peter hastily; and then he smiled, feeling a little foolish for not spotting the joke. "I have a problem I … I was wondering … Well, it sounds so odd really."

The vicar watched him with obvious sympathy. He didn't speak at once, but waited to see if Peter would broach the subject in his own way.

"Grown-ups won't believe it, you see, but I thought you might at least listen and tell me what you think about the *doppelgänger* and the Magic Shop and …"

"Steady on. Suppose you wait till the tea arrives and then you can tell me all about it. I want you to start at the beginning and tell me everything. Don't try to cut it short; that's how important facts get left out."

So, when the tea came and he had nibbled a corner of one of the biscuits Mrs Grant had provided, Peter began his story. He told the whole story of the Magic Shop, about his puzzlement at his friends' behaviour, about Brian's discovery, and finally about Mr Stokes.

When he finished, Mr Grant said: "Tell me, Peter, why you have come to see me."

Peter looked surprised. He stammered, "Well, I thought you would be the best person to ask about such things."

"Did you know I was interested in such matters, that I am actually writing a book on the impact of the occult on modern society?"

"No." said Peter. "I just came here on …"

"An impulse?"

Peter nodded.

"I see," said Mr Grant slowly. "And apart from your

new English teacher – what's his name? Ah yes, Mr Stokes. Apart from him, you haven't mentioned this business to anyone?"

"No," said Peter. "In fact, Mr Stokes actually told us – Brian and me, I mean – not to say anything to anybody."

"What about your father? Have you told him?"

"No. He'd say I was making it up. He doesn't believe in the supernatural."

"You really do believe that something evil is at work, don't you?"

"Yes, I do. I didn't plan to come round here. I was going to Brian's house, but somehow I ended up here."

"I am glad you did. Perhaps there is a special purpose in it. You may have heard it said that God moves in mysterious ways His wonders to perform. I believe that is true."

Mr Grant looked at Peter solemnly for a moment before going on.

"Once, not so very long ago really, there was a time when men believed in the Devil as a being. They thought of him as a creature that walked along dark lanes and stalked through woods, pouncing on poor souls when they least expected it. Well, perhaps that was a little naive. Nowadays, in this age of technology and science, evil is something one reads about in the Sunday papers. It is robbing banks, it's killing people, and swindling old-age pensioners, and stealing – and the law takes care of that sort of evil; or so we are told. But what you have been telling me about is the old type of evil with a capital E – and very powerful it is, too. Once it is unleashed, it is very hard to contain it."

He went to the huge bookcase that ran along the whole width of the study and began pulling out books. He carried them to his desk and began to flip through the pages.

"When I was a young man, I was fascinated by a newspaper account of a black magic scandal somewhere in the south of England. I was interested enough to scour the bookshops, buying several volumes to read up on it. Amongst them I got this." He held up a volume and showed it to Peter. "I found it in an old shop in Salisbury, near the cathedral."

"*Transmigration of the Soul*," said Peter reading the title aloud. "*A treatise by Father Thomas Sullivan.*" Peter looked at the vicar for an explanation.

"He was an Anglican priest who lived in the early part of the nineteenth century. This is a review of all the theories concerning transmigration – that is to say, the passing of the soul from one body to another. He starts with the Ancient Greek, Pythagoras, and comes down through the ages to his own time."

"I've heard of Pythagoras," said Peter.

"Strange isn't it, Peter, to think that the man who invented the theorum you have to learn in geometry also concerned himself with transmigration of the soul? Well, he wasn't the only one. There have been many others since. Sullivan finishes his historical survey with an account of the practices of a group of people living in Winchester at the same time as himself."

"Do you think you can help us?" asked Peter anxiously, feeling that the vicar was beginning to wander from the point.

Mr Grant studied him for a few seconds before saying:

"Yes, Peter, I'll help you. Naturally, there are things I shall have to read up on, and of course with Christmas so close I am very busy right now, but of course I'll do what I can."

Peter looked at him with mounting gratitude and relief in his heart. He was just about to voice his thanks when Mr Grant forestalled him. "Now, Peter, I want you to ask Mr Stokes to telephone me. If we can compare notes it may save valuable time, and time, I suspect, is of the essence for your friends Harry and Jerry. I fancy I may know one or two things that your Mr Stokes is not aware of concerning these matters."

"Oh yes, that's a marvellous idea!" said Peter happily. "As a matter of fact, I'm calling for Brian when I leave here, and we're both going round to Mr Stokes's flat for eight o'clock. He could give you a call tonight."

"No, Peter, tomorrow will do. I need a little time to do some reading first. Ask him to ring me tomorrow. That will be soon enough."

Peter left the vicarage feeling lighter in heart than he had all week. He was glad that he had found a new ally – and fancy the Vicar actually writing a book about black magic! That was an added piece of luck, because not all clergymen believed in the powers of darkness in the old-fashioned sense. As Mr Grant had said, they were living in a technical age and it was understandable that black magic seemed a load of superstitious nonsense to most people, churchmen included.

Peter and Brian walked round the corner of Elm Copse Drive at five to eight. It was a narrow road lined with tall trees and huge Victorian mansions set well back from the road. Here and there a feeble street lamp cast a cold glow on the scene.

They counted off the numbers on the sandstone gateposts as they walked along.

"Number thirteen," said Brian. "Here it is."

They walked up the drive towards the dark outline of the house. The only light visible was a naked electric bulb over the front door. To the right of the archway forming the front entrance was a list of names with bell-pushes by them. Mr Stokes's name was the top one.

After a wait of about a minute, the door opened and the teacher admitted them. He led them up the wide staircase to the top floor.

As they passed along the landing on the second floor, a door was whipped open and an elderly woman popped her gaunt, lined face out and stared at them as they went by.

"Nosy old so-and-so!" muttered Mr Stokes as he walked past her.

Brian and Peter smiled at the old woman, but all they got was a hard stare in return. She was still watching them as they entered Mr Stokes's flat.

The boys were a little surprised to find that the living-room of the flat had been almost entirely cleared of furniture to make room for a large circle which was chalked on the bare floorboards. Inside the circle was a five-pointed star, and at each point of this figure was a symbol and some words in Latin.

"As you can see," said Mr Stokes, "I've been busy this evening. This matter is more urgent than I realized at first."

The boys looked about them with mounting excitement. The unexpected sight of the pentagram brought it home to them that they were on the fringe of something very unusual – possibly frightening.

"Come through to the kitchen. I was just making some coffee and I'm sure you'd like some, wouldn't you?"

They followed the master into a large, bare kitchen and sat down at the table. Meanwhile, Mr Stokes poured coffee into three mugs, added milk and offered them sugar from a cracked basin. It wasn't a very clean kitchen, Peter noted, a little surprised.

When they had settled down and the warm drink had begun to comfort them, Mr Stokes said: "I am afraid your friends are in considerable danger, and I don't mean those two creatures at school. No, your friends are elsewhere, I fear. Those two beings have taken their place."

Brian leaned forward. "I thought something like that might have happened. But why did it happen to Harry and Jerry? And where are they?"

"Well, according to the books I've been looking at, they're now in another world. Some of the writers, though not all, refer to a Shadow Kingdom. It's a world of evil created centuries ago by magical powers to enable certain wicked men to extend their life span far beyond that normally allotted to mankind by his Maker."

Peter's eyes were fixed on the schoolmaster. "Do you mean men have discovered the secret of living for ever?"

"Well, I'd prefer to say they discovered a way of extending their existence. For this continued existence they require the lives of other, preferably young, people."

117

"But how? Why? What do they …"

"I don't know exactly. All I can tell you is that they somehow change places. You see, there are two worlds for them to inhabit. They can come and go as they wish, provided they can obtain the willing co-operation of beings in our world. This they probably do by means of trickery. The innocent victims are used to increase their power in some way I don't fully understand."

"But how can we help Harry and Jerry?" asked Peter. "Surely we can't …"

Mr Stokes silenced him with a raised finger. "We must not mention the word 'can't' in this context. We have to think positive thoughts. Remember, evil is negative; good is positive. We must be the power for good. Do you understand?"

The boys nodded, but not very hopefully.

"It's frightening, isn't it? I'm as scared as you, but I feel I must do something to help your friends. I must! I don't know whether I have the right to ask for your help in this matter, though I need help from someone. If only …"

"I know of someone," blurted out Peter, and told him about the vicar.

Mr Stokes looked hard at Peter, his dark eyes studying the boy's face as though trying to read his thoughts.

Suddenly, he nodded. "I'll call him right away."

"Well, he did say ring him tomorrow," began Peter. "He's frightfully busy this evening, with Christmas and …"

But Mr Stokes was on his feet. "There's no time to be lost. We must act tonight. I'll have to go down to the hall to use the pay phone, as I don't have one of my own. Help yourselves to coffee. I won't be long."

Ten minutes later Mr Stokes returned. His face was glum. "I'm afraid Mr Grant is out on a call. His wife said one of his parishioners is gravely ill and is asking for him. She said she doubted he would be back before half-past nine. Still, she did promise to give him the message. I told her it was urgent and I mentioned your name."

The schoolmaster glanced at his watch several times while he was telling them this and Peter couldn't help noticing.

"What's the matter, sir? You keep looking at your watch. Is it that urgent?"

Mr Stokes nodded gravely. "I'm afraid it is. You see, I've been calculating the time that has elapsed since this changeover occurred, basing it on the visit of your friends to the Magic Shop. If we leave it much longer, there may be a chance that we'll never get them back. What we have to do must be done tonight, at the final phase of the old moon. It can only take place while the moon is in a certain sector of the heavens."

He rose from the table and returned from the living-room with a sheaf of notes.

"You see," he said, jabbing the page with his finger, "by my estimation that only gives us half an hour's latitude. We shouldn't delay the start of our operations beyond ten o'clock, otherwise your friends may be lost for ever."

"You mean they'll never be able to get back to our world? Not *ever*?" said Brian, appalled.

"That is what I understand from the books I studied in the library. It was only when I got back here to the flat that

I began working out the time element. I realized we were right on the edge of the time limit. That's why I set to work and drew the pentagram."

The schoolmaster looked at his watch again. "Well, it's just on nine o'clock. Let's hope the vicar gets here in time to help me. Otherwise, we'll have to call the whole thing off."

Neither of the boys spoke. Nine o'clock came and went, but still there was no sign of the clergyman's arrival.

"You know," said Brian, after what seemed an age, "in the olden days people used to talk about changelings. At least, the country folk did. They used to believe that the fairies carried off their infants and left others in their place. Changelings were always supposed to be rather nasty creatures. It makes you think, doesn't it?"

"Yes. This business has been going on for a very long time indeed. It's odd, though, talking about changelings in the twentieth century, isn't it? But I think that is what we have in Harry's and Jerry's places in school."

It was now twenty past nine and all three were very tense. At last Peter said: "Sir, I'd like to help you if the vicar doesn't show up."

"Me too," offered Brian bravely, though his face looked white and drawn. "We can't just leave Harry and Jerry stranded. We've got to get them back."

"Come on, sir," Peter urged. "Tell us what to do. We'd better make a start soon."

"Well," hesitated Mr Stokes, "with two of you helping, we could try to make a bridge to the Shadow Kingdom, especially seeing that you boys are close friends. You see, there will be some affinity between you, and that will help to establish contact. I suppose it might be all right. There shouldn't be too much risk for you."

"We'll do it, sir. Shall we start right away?"

"I don't know," said Mr Stokes, still holding back on his decision. Then, rising suddenly, he said: "All right, let's get started. We can't afford to wait any longer, though it is a pity Mr Grant isn't here."

The boys followed him into the living-room and watched him as he went round lighting candles. He switched off the two dim electric lamps that had, till now, been the sole illumination in the room. It was darker than ever, the flickering light of the candles being too weak to penetrate very far into the corners of the room. All the light seemed concentrated on the pentagram in the centre of the floor.

"I need you to stand in the centre of the star. I'll be back in a moment. Apparently, it's vital that I am dressed correctly for the ceremony. Face outwards. That's it. Back to back will do fine I should think."

The master left the room and reappeared wearing a long black coat. On his head was a small black circle of cloth, rather like a skull-cap. In his hand he held his sheaf of notes from which he began to recite in Latin. The boys stood and waited.

Nothing happened. They all looked disappointed.

Then Mr Stokes said: "Wait a minute. I've forgotten something."

He walked briskly into a dark corner of the room and emerged from the shadows dragging a tall mirror on a stand. The castors squealed as he drew it over the boards after him. When he had positioned it on the edge of the circle, he returned to the corner and came back with a box in his hand.

"Now, let's start again, and I'll get it right this time. I want you to concentrate on your friends. Try to establish contact with them by thinking of their faces, their appearance in general, or, if you can't do that, try repeating their names under your breath. Have you got that?"

The boys nodded.

"I'm going to use something that will give off a lot of fumes. Don't be alarmed, but I want you to hold your breath. There must be no disturbance of the air within the circle. So, remember, hold your breath while I'm chanting, and think as hard as you can of your friends' names, faces, identities. Your job is to establish a psychic bridge for them to cross and you must call them home across it. Any questions?"

They shook their heads.

"Right, take a deep breath, and we'll begin."

The master stooped suddenly to a candle near the foot of the mirror, and, plunging his long fingers into the box he was holding, scattered some greenish powder into the candle flame and around its base. At once it began to give off a dense brown vapour which smelled horribly of decay.

As the chanting began, Peter saw Mr Stokes stand up and commence a slow gyration. He was no longer holding his notes. They were discarded on the floor.

Peter tried to think of Harry's face, and then of Jerry's, but somehow the sound of the schoolmaster's rising chant interfered with his concentration; besides, his lungs were beginning to hurt as they felt the need for air.

Again he tried to picture his friends and again he failed. "Their names," he muttered. "I must think of their names. I must say them to myself. I must repeat ..." But what was that name he was supposed to hold in his mind? Was it Peter. He had to *think*! Peter? No; it could be Brian. Brian? Well, Brian and Peter then. He must think of those names. He must concentrate hard. *Brian and Peter.*

Brian found his eyes smarting and watering, but he couldn't lift his hand to rub them clear. Through rivulets of tears he watched the revolving figure of the schoolmaster as he began to move along the edge of the circle, spinning as he went. "Peter," he thought. "Peter and Brian." And his lips twitched ever so slightly.

Suddenly, the floor began to vibrate. Brian looked at his feet and then, disbelieving, at Peter's. They weren't there any more; and their legs, too, seemed to be dissolving.

The room continued to vibrate; the walls were shifting, waving, crumbling.

Mr Stokes stopped gyrating abruptly, and stood on the edge of the circle, one hand resting on the frame of the mirror. He was grinning into the mirror and gesturing as though to someone deep within. He seemed to be calling, "Hurry up! Hurry up!" But he uttered no words.

"It's funny I ever thought him a pleasant-looking man," muttered Peter absently, all thought of holding his breath long forgotten. "He's old and ugly. His face is all wrinkled and ..."

Peter's next thought remained unexpressed, for a sudden realization had seized him. He was staring at a face he had seen once before: it had been peering at him through the window the the Magic Shop!

123

He cried out, but a high wind shrieked into the room and shook the walls and floor, and tore at the heavy curtains as though they were mere scraps of muslin with no weight at all. Through it all, buffeted by the tempest, was the old man, staring at them and shaking with laughter.

It was too late and Peter knew it. The wind was tearing at his clothes, knocking him off balance. His last glimpse of the room showed him a dim figure emerging from the depth of the mirror, drawn forth by the old man's skinny hand. He had the oddest feeling that he was looking at a likeness of himself, a likeness that mocked and waved to him, as if it had a life of its own. Finally, the smoke rushed all round him and he felt himself falling, falling, falling ...

CHAPTER 15

A LONG LOST FRIEND

It was difficult not to let the feeling of dismay that took hold of their small party completely engulf them. Alan heard Jerry cry out and, though he also was shocked, he laid a comforting hand on the boy's shoulder, saying: "We mustn't panic, Jerry. We've got to take stock of our situation and plan accordingly. That's what Matthew would expect us to do. Besides, as soon as they realise we're missing, Matthew will send another party to look for us. He'll probably lead it himself."

"I'm s–sorry," stammered Jerry. "It's just that I …"

"I know. We all feel the same. But let's have a look along the passage in the other direction. Bring up the torches so we can see where we're going."

It took forty paces to reach the end of the passageway. In the wall, facing them, was a stout wooden door. Alan held up his hand for silence and then approached the door with caution. Like the others, it was unlocked.

"Well," said Alan, "here goes! We may as well know the worst." So saying, he lifted the latch and pushed back the heavy door.

The room was in every respect like the other cells

further along the corridor. All eyes were instantly drawn to the writhing, changing, shapes of the wall picture, but Alan, conscious of the hypnotic effect of these shifting magical patterns, strode over to it and placed himself in front of it. It was only then, when he was standing with his back to the wall, that he saw the occupant of this solitary cell. He was a man of about Matthew's age, thin and with sparse white hair. He was sitting hunched up on the edge of the crude bunk that served him for a bed. His eyes were fixed steadfastly on the floor between his feet; not even their sudden entrance and the hubbub of voices had caused him to look up. It was as though they did not exist for him at all. From his lips issued a faint tuneless humming, punctuated now and then with an occasional word.

Alan approached the man and touched him gently on the shoulder. Only then did the old man raise his eyes and gaze at his visitors.

The face was impassive, the eyes dark, unblinking. The lips trembled as though struggling with some reluctant word, but nothing was said.

"We are friends," said Alan. "We have come to help you."

For what must have been a good ten seconds the man stared from one to the other of the party in silence; then suddenly his right eye twitched slightly, and a large, slow tear rolled down his grey cheek. He bowed his head and his shoulders shook.

"We mean you no harm. We come to you as friends, to help you. I see that you do not watch the picture as the others do."

The old man looked up, his face wet with tears, his eyes blinking rapidly in the torchlight. Trembling hands reached out to grasp Alan's sturdy ones, and slowly the prisoner drew himself upright until he was standing facing the group. He was very frail, and possibly quite ill.

"I never ..." began the man hesitantly. "I didn't think that ... I never supposed that after all this time I should ever set eyes on ... a friend." And he stood there looking round at their concerned faces. "I can't believe it. Surely, this is a dream, some trick of theirs to torture me in a new and cunning way."

But friendly hands reached out and patted him reassuringly.

"Please," he said, taking a feeble step towards the door, "take me out of this cell."

The effort, however, was too great for him and he collapsed to his knees. Harry and Jerry caught him as he fell and gently pulled him upright again, supporting him on either side. He stood for a while, his head tilted slightly back, panting as though his lungs just couldn't suck in enough air.

At last, he said: "Perhaps I'd better just lie down."

They helped him back to his bunk. "Please, I don't want to be facing that infernal picture," he begged as he struggled to turn himself about; so they helped him and watched him with concern as he settled on his bunk, his chest still heaving.

The seconds ticked by, but no one spoke. It was as if the entire party sensed that they were witnessing something sad, something final.

At last Alan broke the silence. "My name is Alan.

What's yours?"

"Gregory."

"Have you been here long?"

"A lifetime too long. Who knows how time passes down here? There are no clocks; I never see daylight; so it is impossible to gauge the passing of the days."

At his own slow tired pace, Gregory told them that he had arrived at the castle in much the same way as they all had. He had been in his early thirties. Unlike Alan's party, he had been spared the ordeal of the well, only to suffer a worse one. He had become one of the servants of the masters of the castle.

"They treated us like animals," went on Gregory, in a voice so soft that they had to strain to hear him. "They beat us and kicked us and tortured us ... and when we fell down they picked us up and started all over again. It was no use pleading for mercy – they just laughed in our faces and hit us all the harder."

The old man shuddered at the memory of those times, as though trying to shake loose the hold of some frightful picture on his mind.

"I saw things that I never want to think about again; but the most awful thing was the stone-like expression on the face of my master, Metellus, when he was inflicting his cruelties on me. He might have been a statue for all the emotion he betrayed."

"Do you mean that every day they practise some act of cruelty as a ... as a form of entertainment?" said Alan, with a trace of disbelief in his voice.

"Many acts of cruelty occur every day, but, from time to time, they make a special production out of it, as though celebrating some festival or other. Then, of course, no one feels safe, not even them; for on those occasions anyone can be called down into the arena. At these times the entire castle is charged with a sort of energy; you can almost feel it vibrating on the air, like the pulse of a powerful generator. There is a new vitality at work and it shows in their eyes."

Alan shook his head in horror at the thought of the world upstairs in the castle. "What purpose can there be to such a life?" he demanded.

"You might well ask!" said Gregory wearily. "I asked myself the same thing many times as I watched those monsters upstairs, and I have thought about it a great deal since being brought down here."

"And you are still none the wiser?"

Gregory looked at Alan keenly for a moment before answering. At length he seemed to come a decision. He sat up on his bunk.

"I have a theory ..." he said. "I think this entire creation rests on fear. The whole of this world we are now part of seems to depend on terror. It thrives on it. You should see their faces when new arrivals are tossed into the well. Their eyes positively blaze with excitement and their movements are more energetic for days afterwards. Mind you, it's on those days that they quarrel amongst themselves, and sometimes fight. It was then that we servants had to be extra careful; you never knew when they might turn on you."

"But what's this theory of yours?" asked Max.

"Well," said Gregory, taking a deep breath, "before I was brought here I had read about a society of ancients

129

who had learned the secret of eternal life. I believe that this is the essence of the mystery. However, it is an immortality based on evil. Wickedness is the mainspring of their existence: it is pain and suffering and fear that nourish them.

"You see, life is energy; and terror releases vast amounts of energy, more than any other agent. It is this energy that the castle masters require for their own continued existence."

The old man looked from one face to another before going on with his explanation.

"One thing I have learned for certain is that this isn't a normal physical world like the one we all come from."

There were protests that it was all too real, too terrible. How could it not be a physical world?

"You say it is real," countered Gregory, getting excited, "yet what is reality? If I dream that I am being chased by wolves, and I dream that I can feel their hot breath on the backs of my legs, then, while the dream lasts, it's as bad as the real thing, isn't it?"

"But you wake up from a dream," protested Jerry, "and then you know you haven't been harmed. The wolves were simply a dream."

"That's right, but it is only by *waking* that you can escape from the terror. What about the dream that you *can't* wake from? Like this one. Our tragedy is that we don't know the trick of waking ourselves from this nightmare."

"Well," said Alan, "if it is a dream, where are the dreamers? Can we find out where they are?"

"Why not? There is a place, believe me. I have heard

tell of it."

"What? Are you serious?" asked Alan.

Old Gregory looked about him in silence. From the expression on his face it was plain that Alan's last remark had upset him.

After a pause he replied: "Look at me. What do you see? A worn out specimen of a man. How could I fail to be anything else but serious?"

"I'm sorry. I didn't mean it to sound quite like that. It's just that ..."

"I know. You think my talk of dreams and dreamers is proof that I have finally gone mad. It's true that I may have the details a little muddled, but I am deadly serious when I tell you I have spoken to someone who has actually seen the dreamers of our nightmare."

This dramatic statement silenced the little group.

"I told you that terror is the food they need to sustain them. I realized that quite early on. But it was a long time before I realized that although terrible things *seemed* certain to engulf me, they never actually did.

"Time and again I endured the anguish that they intended I should. I have been suspended above flames by a single flimsy thread. I have been pursued around an arena with wild animals snapping at my heels. I have been threatened with death by drowning.

"Then suddenly, one day, I made up my mind to end it all. I decided that I would no longer struggle to survive. I would let whatever fate seemed to threaten me take its course."

The old man smiled bitterly at the memory; and yet there was an air of triumph in that smile, too.

"They had prepared a bed of red hot fire and Metellus said, looking in my direction as he had so often before, that it was time he had a little entertainment. 'Let's put Gregory into the fire and roast him,' he shouted, as if it was a great joke. The other servants, I noticed, shrank back into the shadows hoping to avoid the attention of their masters.

"I wasn't being brave. It was just that I was weary of it all. Anyway, instead of struggling to fend off those tame giants they have up there, I went to meet them. I offered them my arms. I invited them to cast me down into the pit and have done with it once and for all. And do you know what my masters did? Can't you guess?"

No one spoke.

"They howled with anger! They spat and clawed and hissed. And do you know what I did? I laughed in their faces. I laughed in their disappointed faces. And then, before anyone could take hold of me, I leapt down into that inferno and I died."

Suddenly Gregory threw back his head and laughed long and loud. The group looked on, appalled, convinced that the old man had gone completely mad.

But he dried his eyes at last and said: "No, don't be afraid. I'm not mad. I didn't die. That's what I had hoped would happen. Instead, I just stood there in the midst of the furnace looking up at them and laughing. How can the flames of a nightmare devour you? The answer is they can't! And that's why I ended up down here, together with those fools along the corridor."

"But why ...?" began Harry.

"Because I had finally called their bluff. I was no longer

afraid, and without fear they had no nourishment. So I was banished along with the other servants who had witnessed my little act of defiance. From that moment, you see, we were useless to them. They had to replace us with fresh servants, who could still be terrorized. We've been down here ever since."

He gestured contemptuously at the moving pictures on the wall behind him.

"That thing is supposed to keep me quiet down here till the end of my days." He snorted. "Well, it satisfies some people, but not me. I have a mind in here," he said vehemently, tapping his skull, "not a lump of putty."

After a pause, which no one sought to break, Gregory looked at his visitors with a new eye. "I have never seen you about the castle anywhere. How is that?"

"Because we've never been in the castle," Alan told him. "We were all thrown down the well. Even so, I doubt if any of us would have been on the scene while you were serving in the castle. We haven't been here anything like as long as you have."

"You were thrown into the well? You know, I saw that happen many times. You can't imagine just how much the castle masters enjoyed that spectacle when it happened. But how did you get here?"

Alan told him briefly about their small community in the caves, and about Matthew in particular and how it was he who had been responsible for saving them.

"It's all part of the dream," said Gregory when Alan had finished. "You see, even when you're thrown into the well you don't get killed as you expect to; but the terror you feel as you approach the mouth of the shaft must be unbelievable. My masters obviously think it worth losing you for the sake of the energy yield they obtain at the time you're cast into the well. You know, the more I think about it, the more I'm convinced that your best chance of winning your freedom is to challenge them to do their worst and refuse to show fear."

"Look," said Alan, taking Gregory's thin arm, "you must come with us. Matthew ought to hear what you have to say. You could help us a lot, and I think we'll be able to help you. We shouldn't stay here much longer, and, besides, we still have to find a way back into the tunnel."

So, with great difficulty, the old man rose to his feet and, helped by his new allies, took a pace or two towards the door of his cell. Almost at once he stumbled, and if it hadn't been for Jerry's swift reaction he would have fallen and hurt himself. What little colour the old man had had was now drained from his face and his eyes appeared to have sunk back beneath his brows.

"I'm finished," he whispered, in some distress. "I'll never make it. Your arrival here raised my spirits, but I'm afraid my strength has gone."

Alan looked down at the old man. "Don't give up, Gregory."

There was pity in his eyes as he urged the old man to try again. They hoisted him to his feet and, moving step by step, coaxed him into the passage. But old Gregory's legs simply collapsed the moment he was outside his cell door.

"Listen, I'm going fast. My time has come. I know it. My energy is entirely spent ... my continued presence in this corporate dream is no longer required."

Even this short statement seemed to tire him, and the party round him watched sadly as he lay back on the floor, gasping.

"Let's get him back into his cell. At least he can lie down on his bunk," suggested Max.

"No!" said the old man, opening his eyes and staring about him. "Don't take me back in there! I don't want to die in a cell. Out here there is at least *some* measure of freedom."

So Alan and Max knelt down, each taking a hand to comfort the distressed old man.

"There is something I must tell you," whispered Gregory feebly. "I must tell you about the Temple of Dreams."

"Don't tire yourself," said Alan. "When you've rested a while we shall ..."

"There isn't much time left," interrupted Gregory in as urgent a whisper as his failing strength would permit. "I must tell you now. It may be vital to you to know about this place. It's somewhere in the castle – I've never seen it myself, but I have heard about it ..."

Again there was a pause while he rested, but it was plain to those watching that Gregory was desperate to pass on his information, for his eyes roamed restlessly while his breathing returned to a quieter rhythm.

At length he went on: "When I first came down here I shared this cell with a man who believed he was banished from the castle because he'd tried to enter a forbidden place. He hadn't been able to go far because, as he told me, his limbs became immovable, as if weighed down with lead. But the important thing is that he'd seen the entrance and caught a glimpse of the chamber beyond. It was like a chapel inside, but without an altar; and there were rows of draped figures lying on the floor."

"What were they?" Alan asked.

"I don't know for certain, but he told me that he'd never felt such an intense concentration of evil anywhere else in the castle. He was paralysed with fear just looking through the doorway. There was energy there like in a powerhouse."

"What happened?"

"He couldn't remember. All he could say was that he was overwhelmed by a feeling of utter terror and he must have fallen senseless to the floor, because he woke up in this cell. Not long after, he vanished."

"What? Disappeared?"

"You'll see for yourself soon enough," replied Gregory, a strange resigned smile playing about his thin lips.

Suddenly, the old man gasped as a spasm of pain shook his frail body.

"Hold on, old friend," murmured Alan, squeezing the thin hand gently to comfort him.

But even as they watched, the lined face took on a waxen look and then became transparent. To their consternation, the little party found itself watching as the old man literally faded away. For three astonishing seconds Alan was holding a hand that he could see through with increasing clarity. The face, too, was losing substance. Even the pitiful rags that had clothed old Gregory seemed to dissolve in the air as they watched.

In disbelief, Alan felt about him on the floor in the region occupied by the old man, but there was nothing for his hands to touch except the rough texture of the passage floor.

"He's gone! There's nothing left of him!"

CHAPTER 16

DAVID GRANT INVESTIGATES

David Grant stared out across the untidy lawn, watching the rain. He had been thinking about Peter all morning and wondering why Mr Stokes had not contacted him. In fact, he felt distinctly uneasy and he could not explain why. After all, there were several perfectly good reasons why the schoolmaster had not been in touch. Still, it was now the lunch hour, and the phone had remained silent.

"Well," he muttered aloud, "if the mountain won't come to Mohammed, Mohammed must go to the mountain."

He crossed to the red telephone on his desk (that red phone was just the slightest concession on his part to personal vanity) and called Peter's school.

"Mr Stokes, please. My name is Grant. I'm the Vicar of St Andrew's."

Miss Jones, the school secretary, was on the other end and she covered the mouthpiece, looking knowingly at her junior, Doris Lane. "It's someone for Mr Stokes. That's a turn-up for the book, eh?"

She took her hand off the mouthpiece and said: "Will

you hold the line a moment, please? I'll put you through to the Head."

A moment later a voice buzzed in the vicar's ear: "Walker here. Headmaster. Miss Jones tells me you are asking to speak to Mr Stokes."

"Yes. I hope it's not inconvenient, but I thought, with it being the lunch hour, you wouldn't mind my ringing you and asking to speak to a member of staff."

"Not at all, Vicar. It's just that … well, Mr Stokes has left rather abruptly. I got his letter of resignation in the post this morning. Let me read it to you. *'Dear Head'* – not even Headmaster, mark you – *'Herewith my resignation. Yours etc. D Stokes.'*

"There's no reason given, no apologies, and he's certainly not given the statutory period of notice. It's most unprofessional. I have no replacement for him and little chance of getting one before next Easter. I'm really most annoyed."

This would have gone on much longer, for Walker was living up to his nickname of The Talker, but David Grant intervened.

"I'm sorry to hear of your predicament, Headmaster, because it leaves me in a bit of a spot, too. You see, I'm trying to contact the man and I don't have his home address. It's really rather urgent. Do you think you could tell me where he lives?"

"Well, yes, certainly. It's here at the top of his letter: 13 Elm Copse Drive. Listen, Vicar, perhaps you could ask him to give me a call when you see him. I'd very much like a word with him."

David Grant said that he would see to it and put down

the telephone.

He found the house easily enough, but it was not until he had rung the bell for the fifth time that the door was pulled open and a woman with a shopping bag on her arm came out. She smiled politely at the clergyman as he raised his hat and walked into the vestibule. In the hall beyond, a smartly dressed lady with a blue rinse was polishing a hat-stand. In answer to the vicar's enquiry, she pointed upstairs and said: "Top floor."

He climbed the stairs with the pleasant odour of lavender wax polish in his nostrils. On the landing leading to Stokes's door he was met by a thin-faced, elderly lady emerging from her flat.

"I'm looking for Mr Stokes. Is he along here?"

The woman stared at him with her round, dark eyes fixed on his face.

"Is he in, do you know?"

"No, he's not there." She seemed rather vacant. Still staring at him, she went on: "All night he walks the floor. I can hear him, night after night. He never sleeps. Last time I saw him he was rude to me. He always says terrible things to me. He must hate me very much. I'm … I'm afraid of him. I'll be glad when he leaves." And she turned away from the clergyman to re-enter her room. He heard the bolt being pushed home.

He stood looking at the outside of the door for a few seconds, debating whether or not to knock and make further inquiries regarding the schoolmaster, but decided against it.

When he found Stokes's room, the whine of a vacuum

cleaner came from within. He knocked at the door and waited. A plump woman opened the door, her head wrapped in a pink turban, her sleeves rolled up to reveal strong arms.

"Yes? If it's Stokes you want, he ain't here. Left suddenly last night. And what a mess the place is in! And smell? I've come across some smells in my time," she said sniffing as though to drive home her point, "but this fair beats the band. I think it's disgusting."

She spoke with a forceful southern accent and it was plain to see that she was annoyed.

"I've had the window open all morning and you can still smell it. It's a shocker. It's enough to knock a man off his bike a hundred yards away!"

David Grant wrinkled his nostrils. "I see what you mean. It really is vile. Er ... do you mind if I come in?"

"Help yourself, if you can stand the niff in here."

He stepped into the room, looking round for some sign to confirm his suspicions. The plump cleaning lady watched him with curious eyes. As far as she was concerned, anyone connected with the dreadful Mr Stokes deserved to be watched.

"I don't suppose you know where he's gone?"

"No, I do not," she retorted, "and I'm not anxious to be told, either!"

The vicar pursed his lips. "That makes it awkward. You see, I need to interview Mr Stokes on a matter of some urgency. You're certain you've no idea where he's gone?"

"None. He's just hopped it."

He was about to descend the stairs when he heard the woman cry out. He rushed back into the flat.

The woman, looking very shocked, turned thankfully to meet him when he reached the door.

"It gave me quite a turn," she said, pointing to the corner furthest away from the window. "I thought it was a rat."

He crossed the room and stooped to examine the object lying in the angle of the wall.

He picked it up carefully and examined it by the light of the window. It was like a mask made of some fine supple substance he had never seen before. At the top of the forehead was a tousled mat of what looked like human hair. He turned and held it up for the woman's inspection, stretching the fabric of the face as he did so to make it more lifelike. The woman shrieked and back away.

"Heaven save me! It's him! Mr Stokes!"

CHAPTER 17

THE DREAM FACTOR

It was obvious that they were not going to find a way back into the tunnel from the sector they were now in.

"We must try in the other direction," said Alan, and he led them back along the corridor.

They moved slowly, eyeing every inch of the wall as they went. Every cranny, every projection that might have concealed a secret spring was investigated, probed and pressed; but they discovered nothing.

Once past the cells, they found themselves on a steadily rising slope, as though the corridor was bearing them upwards towards the castle. The passage continued in an ever-tightening curve, making it impossible to see very far ahead. Suddenly Max, who was immediately behind Alan, stopped and called out. He pointed to a thin metal ring set into the wall. It was just like the ring that had operated the door mechanism in the tunnel.

"What do you think, Alan?" asked Max.

"Well, we've got a choice. We can either continue following this passage, or we can try to enter the tunnels again. At least in the tunnels we're less likely to meet the enemy face to face. We can remain hidden till it suits us to make a move."

"Besides," said Harry, picking up Alan's earlier remark, "we ought to report back to Matthew."

Everybody agreed that the ring ought at least to be tested to see if it was the key to the tunnel system, so Alan reached out and gave it a cautious tug.

Sure enough there was a low rumbling sound, as if the ground itself was grumbling and complaining. Then came a panicky yell as a section of the stone paving beneath them gave way and two of their party dropped with awesome suddenness through the black oblong that had opened up to swallow them.

The others on the fringes of the group cowered back, clinging to the edges of the passage, listening to the cries welling up from the blackness at their feet. Eventually, far off, they heard a distant splash; then the trap rumbled shut and it was difficult to believe that there had ever been a hole in the floor.

So great was the shock felt by every member of the group, that it was a long time before Alan could urge them forward again.

"I can't help thinking," said Max, looking at Alan earnestly, "of Gregory's words, that it was all an illusion, that we must refuse to be frightened."

"I know what you mean," answered Alan gently, "but he'd been down here a long while and had plenty of time to figure things out."

"Yes," replied Max, "*and* get things wrong! If this is a dream, it's incredibly real."

"And incredibly horrible. Yes, I know," said Alan. "To me those two friends who dropped through the trap a moment ago are just as dead as if they'd been killed by a truck back home. I still can't really accept this talk of a corporate dream, a communal hallucination. But we haven't got time to discuss it now."

"That," said a new voice suddenly, "is a pity; because without at least some understanding of the essence of your being, as applied to this ... this dream factory, you will never escape its toils."

Alan's party found themselves staring at a dishevelled, emaciated figure of a man now dragging himself painfully into view. He was smiling widely.

"I *knew*," he said, "I knew I could feel the strength growing in my bones! I *told* myself that help was on the way. I could feel the energy you were generating."

As he spoke, his eyes were taking rapid count of their party.

"Still," he continued, "I had hoped for slightly greater numbers. You know the expression 'the more, the merrier', I take it? Well, that applies to us prisoners, provided we are all of like mind."

"And are we?" said Alan, a little suspicious.

"We are if you're bent on escape."

Alan nodded. "Look, we've just lost two of our party ..." He gestured to the spot in the floor where the stones had opened up.

The stranger nodded. "I heard your cries. I felt the energy drain out of you. You were like a battery being sucked dry of its power. You see, as you were getting closer I could feel the build-up in my own limbs; my strength was returning at last. I've been stranded here in this passage for what seems an eternity. You can't imagine how elated I was at the thought of joining up with my own kind again. Then suddenly I heard you cry out and I felt the force flood out of me. For a moment I thought you'd all gone."

The man's grey eyes were shining with enthusiasm. He was leaning with one arm against the wall, looking at them, savouring the very sight of them, like a man tasting a banquet with his eyes before he puts the food to his lips.

"I was like you, with a small party, when I first came to this spot; only, in my case, I was left alone in this passage while all my companions were swallowed up. With them gone, I had little power of my own. You see, we're near the castle now and the power of the dreamers is much greater in this region, and it continues to increase the nearer you get to them."

"Dreamers?" said Alan. "Do you know about them?" And he explained what Gregory had told them.

"I think he was right," said the stranger. "This is a dream existence. As he said, it is a corporate dream, a dream we share, a dream we are *all* conscious of. The question is, who controls the dream?"

"The castle people," said Jerry and Harry together.

"Right," said the stranger. "What we have to find out is, can we take over? Can we bend the dream to *our* will? Instead of them controlling us, we must control them. That's the only way we shall destroy this nightmare and free ourselves. You've got to appreciate the nature of the existence you are now experiencing. Without understanding, you'll make foolish mistakes and waste your chances. You may never get a second opportunity to approach the enemy, so you've got to get it right first time."

So saying, he pushed himself upright off the wall and took a stiff stride towards Alan, his hand outheld in a gesture of friendship, a smile on his lips.

"You see," he said, looking about him, "how your coming has built up my strength? Do you realize that when I was on my own I could only crawl along the floor like a snake? I had to drag myself along inch by inch. Now," and he was positively beaming, "I can walk again! My brain is clearer, too, so I can reason and plan."

His joy was so great that he reached out all round him to clasp their hands. "My name is Duncan. You must tell me yours. Let us all join hands," he cried happily, "for the pleasure that is in it!"

And they did, exchanging names and laughing.

"Can you feel the force running through you?" cried Duncan excitedly.

"Yes!" said Alan.

"Yes!" said Jerry and Max and the others.

"Don't let go, then," advised Duncan, "not for a while. We need to feel the energy returning, building up inside us. We need this life force."

"Look!" called out Jerry, pointing up the passage.

There were cries of astonishment as the others saw the object of his attention.

"Come on," called Duncan. "Bring them in! Bring them in!"

They were staring, wide-eyed, at the very couple who had dropped through the trap in the floor only minutes previously!

"No questions," said Duncan, "just bring them in. This

is *our* dream and we must control it!" As he spoke, he was advancing, leading the entire group to the spot where their companions were standing, their own hands outstretched.

The moment they linked up, enlarging the group further, there was a new surge of power. They all felt it.

"Think positive!" said Duncan, taking hold of the hand nearest to his free hand and so completing the circle. "Keep saying to yourself that you are growing stronger by the minute. Say it aloud if you want. It might be a good idea to do that. Yes, shout it! *I am growing stronger! I am in control of my own dream!*"

"There's even more force when all our hands are joined," said Alan. "I felt it really leap into my veins."

They stood for a while, hands linked, chanting together: "*I am master of my own consciousness! I am in control of my own dream! I am growing stronger minute by minute!*"

"If only there were more of us," said Duncan. "Think how much stronger we should be. But as we get closer to the centre of power in the castle, as we must if we're to overcome them, we shall meet increasing resistance, and I'm not sure that we can manage unless we increase our numbers in some way."

"Even so," said Alan, "I think we should press on. We may not be strong enough to conquer the castle people, but we must take the opportunity to find out as much as possible about them and their weaknesses."

"What about Matthew and the others?" objected one of the party. "Shouldn't we go back and tell them what we've discovered? Besides, all those extra people in the chain might give us the extra strength we need."

Alan looked a little impatient. "If we knew how to get back into the tunnels there would be no question of moving on without them. But as it is, we'll just have to make the best of the chances that are offered to us."

"You must have faith in yourself and in us as a group," said Duncan gently, "or you'll weaken us all with your fear."

Inwardly everyone accepted the truth of this statement, but it was far harder to put it into practice.

"Let's get moving, then," said Jerry, with a display of confidence he was far from feeling.

There was a murmur of agreement from the others, and when Alan had issued a final reminder about keeping close together and holding hands at all times, the party set off up the slope towards the castle.

CHAPTER 18

BUILDING THE BRIDGE

Good and kindly man that he was, David Grant was actually rather relieved when his wife told him that her sister Nancy was ill. She was terribly sorry, she informed him, but she would have to leave him to his own resources for a few days while she went to Southport to nurse Nancy. She felt particularly sorry as Christmas was now only a matter of a few days off, but there was nothing else she could do.

"Don't you worry about me, my dear. Of course you must go. I shall be perfectly all right. I'll help you pack." And he did just that.

"Well," said Mrs Grant, turning to him at the door just before running out to the taxi, "it's not as though you're one of those helpless men like that curate we had with us last year. He couldn't boil water without burning it."

"Dearest, you'd better hurry. You've got a train to catch, remember?"

So she pecked him on the cheek and hurried off to Southport.

Once he was alone, the vicar locked the door, took

the phone off the hook, made himself a cup of coffee and then settled down in his study to some serious reading.

For the next few hours he pored over his volumes and scribbled in his notebook. It was eight that evening before he closed the last book with a sigh and went out to the kitchen to cook himself something to eat.

As he trimmed the bacon with his wife's kitchen scissors, he hummed a little tune that sounded suspiciously like *Onward Christian Soldiers.*

"That room in the attic," he muttered as he broke an egg into the hot fat of the frying pan. "It'll do nicely for my purpose. Thank goodness Mary is away."

He was on his way upstairs when he heard the front door bell jangle. He paused in mid-stride, torn by guilt. He ought to go down and open the door. It might be someone in urgent need of help or advice. Then he thought of Peter and Brian. Didn't *they* need his help more than anyone else? After a pause, the bell rang again and then, finally, footsteps grated on the gravel drive as the caller walked away.

David Grant continued up the stairs to the attic. Once there, he produced his notebook, a piece of chalk and a length of string from his capacious pockets.

"Let me see. A circle here to begin with ..." And so he started to work, muttering to himself and looking frequently at his notes to check dimensions, angles, quotations. It was a complex diagram involving circles within circles, crosses within crosses, stars within stars. Several of the quotations were in Classical Greek; some were in Latin.

"This is the most powerful of all the signs according to the books. The major authorities all agree. However, the bridge can only last for twelve hours. After that it'll break. If it does break, then one thing is certain: I shan't be here for the Christmas services."

He walked up and down the room, checking the diagram carefully, and then checking again.

"Now, just one more thing. An object of purest silver, ideally something that will fit readily in the hand and is easy to carry around."

After a moment's thought, he strode from the room, to return moments later with a silver medallion belonging to his wife. It consisted of an old American dollar threaded on a silver chain. It had belonged to Mary's mother, given to her by some long-dead pioneering uncle when she was a little girl. The coin was pure silver.

"If I put this round my neck, I can take hold of the coin whenever I need to without fear of dropping it."

Once that was done, he locked the door, lit a candle and then stuffed his notebook into his pocket. Taking a deep breath, he stepped into the circle. Standing erect, each foot touching a point of the star within the star, right in the centre of the design he had drawn, he began his incantation.

After a while the floor began to vibrate. From far off came the howling of a mighty wind and the calling of many voices. Walls crumbled, bricks flew apart in silent explosion, plaster and timber separated and he felt himself sucked out into space. The winter stars burned fiercely for an instant and then dimmed suddenly into a spinning blackness that engulfed him.

In his heart had he really believed in all this magic nonsense? Hadn't he half expected it to fail? Now, here he was … where?

CHAPTER 19

A STRANGE SORT OF DUEL

"How *can* you control a dream?" asked Jerry, who had been deep in thought for some time. "It doesn't seem possible."

"This isn't like being at home in your bed, Jerry," replied Alan. "Here we're part of the enemy's dream. We're elements of a huge illusion, and we're controlled by the dreamers – whoever they are. We have to break the dream pattern somehow."

"I've been thinking about that," interrupted Duncan.

"And?"

"Well, as I see it, by uniting our efforts like this, we can distort the events of the enemy's dream. Our two friends, for instance, were brought back from the pit. That was something the dreamers never intended to happen. You can count on that."

"But we didn't consciously do anything to bring them back," said Alan. "We thought they were dead or trapped for ever."

"True," admitted Duncan, "but the thing to remember is that it was an example of the dreamers losing control. I suspect that at this very moment they're having some bad vibrations in their eternal sleep. All the same, we must watch out, because they will fight back, and, near their own den, they'll have much greater power."

Not long afterwards, they came to a flight of steps which led up to a heavy door set in the rock.

Forgetting their circumstances momentarily, Alan detached himself from the human chain saying: "I'll go up and see if it's locked."

But the moment he lost contact with the others, he staggered to the floor.

"My legs," he croaked, "they've given way! I can't … move … them."

It was Duncan who saved the situation by leaning forward and offering his own hand to link Alan back to the chain. As soon as the chain link was established Alan seemed to recover and was able to regain his feet.

"We must never risk that happening again," said Duncan. "We'll have to maintain contact at all times."

"It will be awkward to move about quietly if we have to hold on to one another all the time," said Max. "Can we manage like that?"

"It seems as though we shall have to."

Again Alan went towards the steps, but this time he was holding on to Jerry's hand, who in turn was linked to the others. He put his ear to the door.

After listening carefully for a couple of minutes, he looked back and nodded. Slowly, he lifted the latch and pulled the door towards him.

They emerged on a high gallery which overlooked a large, stone-flagged hall. To everyone's surprise the hall itself was lit by tall windows, through which they could see into the courtyard beyond.

"The logic of the dream," murmured Duncan, standing between Alan and Harry. "One moment we're underground, the next we're high up on a ledge."

Harry said nothing. He was staring with startled eyes at two figures in the centre of the hall.

Then Jerry saw them too. "That's Peter down there! And isn't that Smithy with him? What are they doing here?"

"The same as us, I suppose," said Alan, after warning him to keep his voice down. "Friends of yours?"

The boys nodded.

By now the entire party had emerged, and they were standing in line abreast peering over the low balustrade into the hall, watching the events taking place below.

Round the hall, on all sides, except for a space near the huge wooden doors, ran a line of tables at which sat row upon row of the castle people. Every eye in the hall was fixed on the two boys in the centre of the floor. Each was held firmly in the grip of one of the giant retainers.

A man was speaking in a low, emotionless voice and Harry gasped as he recognized the young man with the ebony wand, the man who had ordered Lucan to drop him into the well.

"That is Metellus," murmured Duncan, looking down with glittering eyes. "I have cause to remember him."

Harry was about to say something, but the meaning of the words drifting up to his ears froze him.

"We shall see how they fare against Molaf, I think. That should give us some sport – and Molaf, too, I shouldn't wonder. You can release them, Lucan. They won't be going far." Metellus laughed quietly at his joke, and there was a ripple of amusement from those about him.

"Charging their batteries," said Duncan. "That's how it is done. There's nothing like a bit of terror for doing that."

"We can't just stand here," protested Jerry.

"We haven't got much option," said Alan. "We're too high up on this gallery to be able to interfere."

A sudden increase in the chatter below prevented further argument. All eyes turned towards the great doors which were creaking slowly open. Through them came a dwarf mounted astride a huge dog.

"That must be Molaf," said Alan, eyes fixed on the little man who was wearing a large pointed cap with an enormous feather in it. This he removed and, with a mocking bow, flourished it in the exaggerated manner of a French nobleman.

"At your service, Metellus. You have a task for me?" He twiddled his fingers with feigned delicacy.

Metellus nodded, eyes aglitter with anticipation.

Again Molaf bowed. Then, digging his heels into the flanks of his mount, he brought his steed down the shallow flight of steps towards the boys.

To mounting applause from the spectators, he circled the boys twice, looking at them carefully. Then he sniffed and spoke directly to Metellus.

"Not much of a challenge for me, Metellus, are they? I can stick them like a couple of piggy-wigs before you can bat one of your handsome eyelids, my lord. Have they weapons?"

Metellus shook his head. "Do your opponents ever have weapons?"

"No … no, they don't, but they are usually a little more mature. They usually offer a better prospect of entertainment for me, my lord, wouldn't you say?"

"Perhaps. But these are what we have to offer. Of course, if you'd rather not oblige us today, I can have them cast into the snake-pit."

"My lord, my lord! Please don't be hasty. I was merely ruminating." Again he twiddled his fingers daintily. "I shall be happy to oblige." So saying, he urged his steed up the hall to the far end.

To Peter, down on the floor of the hall, it seemed that the grotesque nightmare he and Brian had been sharing since the schoolmaster had tricked them would never end. Facing this weird little monster, he wondered just how he and Brian would fare.

Suddenly Brian was pushing something into his hand. "Use the catapult, Peter. You'd be better at it than me."

"What about ammunition?"

"I've got three marbles. That's all, I'm afraid."

"Listen, then. Stick close by me till he's almost on top of us, then, when I give you the word, dive to your right. I'll go to the left. That's the best I can think of right now."

An unearthly stillness fell on the room. Molaf had wheeled round to face them and was drawing from his belt a long thin dagger. It glinted murderously in the sunlight that slanted through the tall windows.

With beating hearts the boys watched Molaf spur his steed forward into a charge, the little man bent low along the animal's back, sword-arm stretched out in front.

Suddenly, there was no time to use the catapult, for

Molaf's dagger was scything the air in a glittering arc close to his ear. Peter barely managed to fling himself out of the way.

A roar went up as throats on all sides expanded with laughter and comment.

Peter scrambled to his feet to see the dwarf hastily remounting the dog, for he too had taken a tumble in his eagerness to slice the boys with a classic double stroke, one for each of them. He had missed both. There was dust on his fine blue jacket and he resented it.

Over his shoulder he glowered at Peter. "I'll have you this time, Monsewer! No one makes Molaf look foolish."

"Except Molaf," called Brian, cheeks aflame.

The little man froze with ice-cold anger. Fixing Peter's friend with his dark eyes, he nodded slowly, threateningly.

Meanwhile, Peter was taking off his jacket. He let it fall at his feet; then, calmly, he fitted a marble into the pouch of the catapult. For some reason he did not understand, his nerves had stopped twitching, his fingers had become efficient once again, and he was able to watch his opponent without trembling.

Molaf was away at the top of the hall by now, and when he turned his mount he must have hurt it, for the animal yelped and sprang forward across the arena, snarling as it came.

Peter held his aim as long as he dared and then let fly, with the dog some ten yards off. Molaf's broad head, his target, Peter missed, but the marble caught the dog a glancing blow on the muzzle, causing it to shy away suddenly, unseating its rider.

Down went Molaf in a cloud of dust. The air was

jagged with the shouts and curses of Lucan and the other retainers. The castle people merely watched, smiling thinly and without humour.

Molaf stood there, red murder in his heart, watching his dog-mount running along the far side of the hall, well out of reach. He was uncertain whether to pursue it and try to remount (thus risking making a bigger fool of himself if he should have trouble capturing the dog), or to advance on foot and deal with his victims face to face. The choice was not left to him. At the snapping of Metellus's fingers, the big double doors were opened and the dog fled through the gap, howling as it went.

Molaf's face was set, the deep lines running downwards from the side of his nose giving him a haggard look. As he came forward he began to toss the dagger from hand to hand, growling: "This knife is going to slice your liver. I'm going to cut it out and toast it before your eyes. First you," he said pointing at Peter, "then you, fat boy. I shall particularly enjoy slicing *your* liver!"

Keeping an eye on the advancing Molaf, Peter snatched up his coat and held it in his left hand. A second later Molaf leapt an incredible distance and the dagger point was lunging up at Peter's ribs.

It was the coat that saved him, acting as a cushion to some extent, though the blade did actually slice his wrist a little, causing Peter to cry out and drop the catapult.

But Molaf was off balance too, and without thinking of the danger, Brian charged him, knocking him flat.

Peter turned and dropped his coat over Molaf's head, unsighting him. A desperate struggle ensued to wrest the vicious dagger from the dwarf's hand. His strength, however, was astonishing.

"I can't hold him," panted Peter. "Make a break for it – now!" And they ran off in opposite directions.

It was Brian who scooped up the catapult this time, and Peter tossed him one of the two remaining marbles. Molaf, however, appeared unaware of the danger. All he was concerned about was catching up with Peter.

"He's had it now," said Lucan to the creature standing next to him. He appeared to be expressing a professional interest in the contest. "Molaf will hunt him down; then he'll get the other one. You just watch. I've seen it many times."

Brian was nowhere as calm as Peter had been as he tried to fit the marble into the soft leather pouch. His hands were shaking and his fingers were clumsy as he pulled back the sling to take aim at the broad, dark head of the jabbering dwarf.

Molaf, meanwhile, was telling the spectators just what he was going to do to the boys by way of slicing them and cutting them. He was in a state of intense anger, and little flecks of white foam flew from his lips.

He was still prattling on when the marble struck him on the side of the head, causing him to scream with pain. He looked about him, puzzled by the fact that both of his victims were still some way distant from him. The concept of the catapult was obviously unknown to him. There was uproar in the hall as Lucan and the other servants clamoured for more action from Molaf.

"Get it over with, Molaf!" called Metellus, his voice thin with distaste. Where was the terror in all this, he asked himself. He wanted a greater energy yield than this!

It was Duncan standing next to Harry who first noticed the panelling moving behind Metellus's chair.

"Look!" he hissed. "There, behind Metellus! In the wall. Do you see it?"

"There's someone standing there," exclaimed Alan. "Do you see him, Harry? It's Joshua!"

Suddenly, a file of people clambered out through the gap in the panelling, each person linked to the next by hand held in hand. Above all the din that arose in the hall came Matthew's clear tones, urging his party on. Soon they were spilling across the floor, surrounding Peter and Brian, protecting them.

"Join hands!" called Matthew. "Join hands!"

All at once the air in the great hall became dark. It was like a winter storm brewing above the heads of the opposing factions.

"Lucan!" screamed Metellus, his voice straining to rise above the flood of shouting and movement. "Seize them! Seize them!"

But the giant stood rooted to the flagstones, as though paralysed.

"Seize them, Lucan! I command you. You are my creature. Do as I command you!"

A slight shudder ran through the giant's frame, but he did not respond to his master's order.

"Come on," Duncan urged. "Do you see what is happening? There is a balance of power. We *must* get down there and join the newcomers." And before anyone could stop him, he leapt off the high gallery.

It was just like a dream. Instead of plummeting to his death, Duncan dropped slowly to the ground in a controlled descent, landing directly on top of the mesmerized Molaf, who seemed to implode and disappear.

In a matter of seconds, Alan and the rest of his party dropped down to the great hall and were linking hands with Matthew's party.

The air rang with cries of recognition. It was a wonderful moment. As each new ally was linked into the chain, there was a fresh surge of power.

"We're winning!" called Matthew. "They can't hold us. See how their creatures are fading away!"

And it was true, for Lucan was now a mere shadow staining the air. The gloom that had hovered over the warring factions was dispersing. Metellus and his white-faced castle people were fleeing. Soon Matthew and Alan and their supporters had the great hall to themselves.

It was Alan who brought a halt to their rejoicing. "We've only just begun!" he cried. "We must follow them to their source of power, to the Temple of Dreams. We must destroy them before they build up their strength again!"

"Yes," shouted Matthew. Then he pointed towards the side of the hall. "Look there, at those shadows!"

"What are they?" Jerry asked nervously.

"They're what's left of those creatures of theirs. Perhaps they aren't entirely gone. Perhaps they can be recalled if the castle people regenerate themselves. Maybe they will only completely vanish when we succeed in destroying the dreamers who conjured them up in the first place."

With cries of jubilation their party burst out of the great hall and spilled along the corridors. Now only one or two remembered to clasp hands, but it did not seem to slow the progress of the others.

"Why is that?" asked Harry, jogging alongside Jerry and Peter, with Brian trotting on the far side.

"Because," said Duncan, leading them to the foot of a wide staircase and beginning to mount, "there's more of us than of them now – and *we're* in control of the dream at last. Our spirits are high, and our confidence is growing by the minute. Let's hope it's enough to sustain us."

"Is that why Brian and I were able to move freely in the hall?" said Peter.

"Possibly. After all, there were rather a lot of us waiting in the wings, so to speak."

By now they had reached the top of the staircase and were hurrying along the corridor, ahead of the group.

Alan opened a door on his right. It was empty.

"Try the next."

It was the same again, and the same with the one beyond that.

Suddenly, Alan, who was ahead of the rest, halted in his tracks. He remained still for an instant, arms spread wide as though reaching across the corridor, a slight tremor running through his body. Then, all at once, his entire body glowed with a green fire and he vanished.

CHAPTER 20

THE TEMPLE OF DREAMS

David Grant swam upwards through a crystal fountain, the spangling water winking and flashing as he turned in the uprush of the current. Suddenly, it was not a fountain any more, for the water was still and he was the only moving thing in it. Looking up towards the light, he saw that he was a long way from the surface, but he was rising fast and a few seconds later he was emerging from the pond, walking out of it as though it was the shallowest of pools.

As he stood on the edge, he looked down at the surface and saw himself perfectly mirrored there. There was not a ripple anywhere; nor was he wet from his enforced swim. Indeed, he found it difficult to believe it was anything but a mirror, so perfect was the sheen upon the surface of the liquid.

"So," he murmured to himself, looking about him, "this is the end of the journey?"

He was standing in the middle of a large, bare chamber, circular in shape, and lit only by a ring of tall black candles which were fixed on silver spikes set into the stone flags. On the wall hung a vast black banner with a full moon worked in silver thread in its centre.

He stared at it for some time. "A fitting emblem, I suppose," he muttered as he studied it. "The moon has long been the talisman of the workers of darkness."

His fingers reached up to touch the medallion at his neck, and the contact comforted him greatly.

He approached a heavy wooden door and had hardly opened it more than an inch or two when he felt a shockwave hit him. He was forced back and left numb, breathless, and dazzled.

Again his fingers sought the comforting silver disc. When his senses cleared, he found himself staring at the faint outline of a young man. The apparition, as he supposed it to be, seemed in a deep trance. When he reached out to touch it, he found nothing to take hold of.

He was more disturbed than alarmed, more uneasy than afraid. There was something in the countenance of this young man that seemed honest and gentle.

"Perhaps," he murmured, looking back at the image, "I shall be able to help you, too, when I have done my other work."

At the doorway he positioned himself so that he could look through the gap between the edge of the door and the door-jamb. This time there was no great energy wave to meet him, though he could still feel some sort of resistance.

Holding the silver dollar in his fingers, he pushed the door wide and stepped across the threshold.

It was like standing in the great hall of a castle, or the chancel of some ancient cathedral. High on either side, suspended from poles, were rows of antique banners, so old that all colour had long since faded from the fabric. In some cases, even the material had dropped away, leaving only the delicate tracery of the golden thread.

The chamber was illuminated by no more than a couple of candles fixed in brackets on the stone walls. Wide margins of shadow ran down either side of the chancel and wedges of gloom intersected at intervals where the massive pillars obstructed the wan glow of the feeble lights.

In the shadows, scarcely discernible, was a long row of stone tablets stretching away into the darkness at the far end. Each tablet was mansize, and each one supported something long and gaunt and covered with a drape of some sort.

It was with a trembling step that he advanced further into this room. As he moved, he became aware of a faint whisper, a rustling on the still air. It seemed to run on ahead of him, and then sweep round and scamper over the walls and wing up into the hidden rafters. With each faltering step the whispering increased, but the words, if words they were, remained unintelligible. For the first time in his life, David Grant knew real terror, and as his terror mounted, he felt his limbs weakening and his spirit quaking within him. His head sank to his chest as the energy drained out of him.

Suddenly, the chamber filled with light as torches appeared between the pillars. Strong, defiant voices echoed clearly from the walls as the marchers came on towards him.

Then he heard someone calling, over and over again: "Reverend Grant! Reverend Grant! Is it *really* you? It's me, Peter. Peter Linton!"

Suddenly, David Grant felt his hands seized and knew what it was to experience the energy force flooding into his body. The terrible lassitude that had begun to overwhelm him drained away.

In the background, jubilant voices were shouting: "This is it! We've found it! This is the Temple of Dreams!"

"So this," said Matthew, looking about him amazement, "is the centre of the corporate dream. And now, at last, we are in control of it."

Torch in hand, he crossed the chamber to examine the draped forms on the stone tablets – and recoiled in horror as he uncovered the first of them.

Beneath the drape lay a figure, but a figure so ancient that the flesh had long since petrified: all that remained was a hideous, staring skeleton with the merest covering of flesh and sinew. Each shape was the same; each face had its own special grimace or leer, each glassy eye its own peculiar glint.

"So *that* is what true wickedness looks like," said David Grant, staring down at a grinning corpse. "Pray God I never look upon such a thing again." And he turned away with a shudder.

"These," said Matthew, "are the dreamers. These are the ones who have controlled our lives for so long. Now we have them at our mercy."

"Mercy?" said Duncan. "There can be no question of

mercy. They must be destroyed, and it must be done now."

"But they're corpses!" exclaimed Harry. "How can they be the dreamers? They're dead!"

In a sudden lull in the conversation around him, Harry's voice rang out loud and clear, echoing round the chamber, and bouncing back eerily out of the shadows. For a moment no one else spoke. Then the whispers that had startled David Grant became audible to the others, and there wasn't one of them whose blood was not chilled.

There was a sort of urgent ferocity to the sound and it was growing in power.

"Look!" cried a voice from the far end of the room.

"What is it?" called anxious voices. "What's the matter?"

Matthew, striding up the hall, halted by the frightened man and saw for himself. Two of the figures on adjoining slabs had somehow linked hands.

"They must have been like that for eons," he said reassuringly. "See, the very bone has fused!"

"No. They weren't like that when I first looked at them." There was an edge of hysteria in the voice, and that hysteria travelled down the hall.

Almost at once there were more shouts of "Look here!" and "They must be moving!"

Back strode Matthew, anxious himself now, for he could feel the confidence leaking away from his party.

A man on the fringes of the group swayed heavily and toppled to the floor. Then a woman fell forward, followed by one of the young girls.

"Join hands!" called Duncan. *"For God's sake, join hands!"*

Matthew, too, took up the cry, but there was a continuing rundown of power and more of the party fell unconscious to the floor.

Harry, standing next to Jerry and Peter, noticed with a shudder what he was convinced was a new smile on the face of one of the dreamers.

Matthew was growing desperate, for he could see what was happening and yet was unable to stop it.

"We *must* destroy them," urged Duncan. "Help me, Vicar. Help me find something to strike them with!"

David Grant stepped forward, his hand clenched upon the silver disc that he had removed from his neck. Now was the time for the supreme test of his chosen formula. If he had selected unwisely in his haste, then he and all who depended on him would be lost; for he could feel the power of evil beginning to surge around him.

Approaching the first figure, he stumbled as a wave of dizziness flooded his brain. Duncan, however, was there at his side, steadying him, and he recovered sufficiently to lay the silver medallion flat upon the two bony wrists that were now clasped one upon the other.

The moment it touched those grotesque fingers the silver coin glowed, so brightly indeed that it dazzled all who looked at it. It was like a white hot mirror and it sent out a beam of light high into the roof, dispelling for a moment the blackness crowding there.

Suddenly, there came a sound like the cracking of a stick, then another, and another, as the sound travelled along the hall.

"What's happening?" called Peter.

"The hands! Look at the hands!" shouted Joshua.

"The hands are shattering!" cried Brian, hope ringing in his tones.

And it was true. All along the chamber the skeleton fingers, which had so recently and mysteriously formed the gruesome chain linking creature to hideous creature, had splintered, and fragments of bone were littered about the floor.

Almost immediately, one of the party, who had been lying unconscious on the flags near the great door, stirred and sat up.

David Grant, still holding on to the chain of the medallion, felt the floor tilting, saw the light fading in front of his eyes, but only for a few brief seconds. As soon as he felt the touch of supporting hands about him, the energy flowed back into his mind and his vision cleared.

Looking down at the skull of the figure before him, he was astonished to see a network of fine lines running across the surface of the bone. Little by little, the cracks widened until the structure of the skull began to fall apart and crumble to a dull brown dust.

"The castle people are decaying," cried a voice some way down the all. "They are destroyed!"

A great cheer went up. The spirits of the party rose in triumph, and all around happy voices chattered and babbled.

Their elation deserted them as rapidly as it had arrived, and a dismayed silence fell on the room.

"What's the matter?" asked Joshua, peering about him.

"There is something, or someone, near the door," whispered Peter, his fear returning.

Old Matthew stepped closer to David Grant. "Can you make out what it is down there?"

"They ... they appear to be people." He hesitated, blinking his eyes in an effort to see more clearly. "They appear to be, well ... like Roman senators, judging by their robes."

The vicar turned his face away suddenly and shut his eyes, as though deeply disturbed. When he spoke again, his eyes remained closed.

"Their faces ... Their eyes ... there is such a smouldering hatred in them. I can hardly bear to look." His breath shuddered in a long deep sigh in his chest. Then he opened his eyes and his gaze was resolute. "I must finish this thing."

Standing tall and erect, Matthew on one side of him and Joshua on the other, he strode towards the ghostly throng hovering near the door of the great chamber.

When he was within ten feet or so of them, he called in a loud voice: "Go from here to the place prepared for you and all creatures like you. I command you to leave this place and trouble us no more!" And as he spoke, he held aloft the silver disc, so that it cast its dazzling beam on the phantom gathering.

For one long, terrifying moment, Matthew and his party saw the outlines of the castle people clearly illuminated as they stood near the entrance. Then their ghostly robes began to smoulder and little tongues of green flame licked at the edges of their togas.

The last thing Harry recalled seeing was the pale, staring face of the young man called Metellus looking back at him. Then the light dimmed and they were gone.

CHAPTER 21

SURPRISE LANDING

They went down, under David Grant's supervision, into the crystal pool. The minister stood on the edge of that polished mirror, watching them swimming down through the clear liquid. Down and down they went, one behind another, the weaker ones helped by the stronger ones, but always downwards in their progress.

At last it was his turn; then he remembered the apparition he had seen when he had first climbed out of the pool: the young man. Surely he had not been one of the castle people?

The vicar looked around, but there was no sign of him. Eager though he was to follow the others, he felt uneasy, as though he was abandoning a friend.

"I must at least search for him," he murmured.

So, with anxious tread, he turned back from the edge of the pool and walked towards the doorway.

It was really more like flying than swimming. Peter found that he could breathe quite normally, despite the fact that he appeared to be underwater. Just once, he turned and looked back towards the surface, but all he could see was a blinding sunlight that suffused the surrounding element with its golden warmth.

Then, inexplicably, he saw looking down on the castle from above. As he watched, he saw a blinding flash, and the roar of thunder that followed it seemed to shake the entire building. A vivid tongue of flame licked up the side of the great hall and flames spurted out of first one window, then another. Suddenly, the huge tower over the gate, where Harry and Jerry had first entered the castle, began to totter and then crumble. It fell with a roar that shook the heavens.

The air was full of flying debris, and smoke rolled across his vision causing him to lose sight of some of his companions. Once or twice, Peter caught a glimpse of figures hurtling past him in the opposite direction. Could that writhing figure be Harry? Or that one Jerry? They were gone in an instant but he had caught the likeness. He looked back to follow their flight, but they were mere specks by now. And Harry was right beside him; so were Jerry and Brian.

"*Doppelgängers*!" mouthed the plump boy beside him. "Did you see them?"

The next thing that Peter was aware of was a sound. It was a high-pitched screaming and definitely feminine.

He opened his eyes and blinked them with surprise. He was standing on a thick red carpet. In front of him was a plump woman holding a large pink hat in her pudgy fingers. Behind her was a woman who looked like a shop assistant. Both women were staring at Peter with eyes like prize blue marbles.

"He … he came out of that mirror!" screeched the woman with the hat. "I was looking at myself in the mirror and he stepped right out of the glass! On dear! I think I'm going to faint …"

And she did, leaving the assistant, who felt like fainting herself, to struggle with her heavy bulk.

There was no time for explanations. Peter took to his heels and pelted out of the Millinery Department, right through Soft Furnishings and down the escalator. Thirty seconds later he was on the pavement looking up at the sign about the huge window.

"Lewis's?" he muttered. "What am I doing here?"

At that moment two more figures scuttled out through the doors.

"Harry! Jerry!"

"Eh? What? Oh, thank goodness!" said Jerry, panting. "They nearly caught me. When I opened my eyes, I was standing right behind an assistant, next to the till. She gave an awful yell. I think she thought I was after the cash. She gave me a terrible fright. I didn't wait to explain, I can tell you."

"Where's Brian?" asked Peter. "Have you seen him anywhere?"

The others shook their heads. They'd been too concerned with their own predicaments to think of the other boy.

Along the pavement towards them came Ann, with her little brother Timmy. The boy was sniffling and rubbing his head.

"He fell and hurt himself," explained the girl, "but he's all right. It's not serious. Come on, now, Timmy. Cheer up. You'll soon be home with Mummy."

"What happened to you?" asked Harry. "Where did you land?"

"Right up on the fire escape. That's how Timmy came to fall. He was frightened of the height and he stumbled on the iron staircase."

"I'm starving," said Harry. "I feel as if I haven't eaten for days."

"Me too," said Jerry. "Has anyone got any money? Perhaps we could find a snack bar."

But they were all penniless.

"Listen," said Peter, "we ought to prowl around and see if we can find some of the others, don't you think?"

An hour later they had assembled about twenty of their companions, and a peculiar group they were, too. Passers-by certainly regarded them with curiosity, turning to stare and comment on the rags some were wearing, and the wild condition of their hair.

"If you ask me," said one comfortable-looking woman stepping our of her Rover saloon at the edge of the pavement, "they're those drop-outs you keep reading about in the papers. Home, James. You can pick me up at the theatre entrance at four-thirty." And she swept away along the pavement on her high heels.

Of Matthew there was no sign, nor did they find Duncan, the tall stranger they had met in the passage beneath the castle. They didn't see Joshua, either.

"Well," said Ann, "perhaps they landed somewhere else. It's possible."

"What about Mr Grant?" asked Jerry. "We haven't seen him either."

"No," said Peter, feeling a little uneasy. "He said he would wait till last. He had to, he said, to keep the bridge open."

"Bridge?" asked Harry. "What do you mean?"

"Only what he said. He had to keep the bridge open."

"But there wasn't a bridge. I didn't see one. Did you, Jerry?"

"I think he was speaking metaphorically," said Ann. "He didn't mean a bridge with stones and girders. He must have been referring to a link of some sort, a link between the two worlds."

The others were silent. Some of Peter's anxiety had rubbed off on them.

"I hope he's all right," said Peter. "It was me that got him into this business."

"It's just as well you did," observed Harry. "Without him we'd all still be trapped in the castle." He looked round him and up at the high frontage of the department store. "I wonder if this is where the castle is … in some other dimension, I mean."

"The castle was destroyed," reminded Peter. "Didn't you see it?"

Harry nodded. "I was just wondering, that's all."

"You'll never know the answer to that," said Brian, coming out of the shop door to join them. He was smiling broadly and eating a cream bun.

"Hey, give us a bit!"

"Where have you come from?"

"Who gave you that?"

He was hemmed in by questions on all sides.

"I simply found myself in the food department. A man

came up to me and said, 'Are you the new lad? Well, don't stand there. Help unload the van.' And he took me to the loading bay and set me working with the van driver unloading the trays of cakes."

After the others had commented with some envy on his good fortune at being placed right next to meals on wheels, so to speak, Peter asked his friend if he had seen anything of Mr Grant.

"No," replied Brian, "but I've just seen Max come pelting out of Men's Underwear with a store detective hot on his heels. I think he got away, though."

"You know," said Jerry, "I'm sure we'll find he's safe and sound back at the vicarage. Don't worry, Pete."

After waiting about a little longer, the party began to split up and drift homewards, each of them anxious in his own way to find what was awaiting him at home when he got there.

When Harry walked in, his mother said: "Well, where's the loaf, then?"

Then she looked at him more sharply. "What *have* you been doing to your clothes? Good grief! You've been in an accident. Are you all right, son? Tell me what happened."

So, to avoid shocking his mother further, Harry was compelled to tell a few fibs. But it was obvious to him that he had not been missed. He would have been puzzled if Peter and Brian had not previously warned him what might happen.

Peter found that there was no one at home when he arrived, so he simply let himself in with his key and went upstairs to wash and change.

Brian got a clip over the ear for tearing his pants, but he

managed to survive that.

Jerry, tripping over a jutting kerbstone, fell headlong into a large puddle on the edge of the pavement halfway along his street. When he reached home, his mother was so busy telling him off for getting himself into such a mess that she didn't notice the other things about him that might have been awkward for him to explain.

It was, however, David Grant who had the roughest homecoming. He found himself wandering around outside the vicarage, his clothes in shreds, his face blackened with soot, and minus his shoes. All around him on the lawn were strewn bricks, pieces of rafter, slates, huge chunks of rock and a great deal of plaster dust. Considering that the house itself was in no way damaged, he was at a loss to explain it.

To make things worse, his wife was even at that moment alighting from her taxi at the gate. She turned and stared at him in utter bewilderment.

Finally, emerging from the shrubbery, was a pale-faced young man, namely Alan, carrying the torn remnants of a huge black banner with a silver disc embroidered on its centre. The silver moon was somewhat scorched and blackened.

"David," said Mrs Grant, staring at her husband, "what on earth have you been doing while I've been away? And just before Christmas, too!"

"Well, my dear," he began, "it's like this …"

A few weeks later, Peter overheard his mother talking to Mrs Sellers.

"Your Harry seems like his old self again, doesn't he?"

"Yes, I'm glad to say. He was quite peculiar for a time, and *so* bad-tempered. I was awfully upset when Mrs Higgins told me he'd been hitting their Ronnie. He gave him a terrible black eye. I mean to say, that wasn't like our Harry, was it?"

"No. Mind you, Peter went a bit funny for a while. He's back to normal now, but I was beginning to get a bit worried about him."

Mrs Sellers was shaking her head. "You wonder what gets into them at times, don't you?"

"Yes. Mind you, I blame television. I was saying to Mrs Alexander only the other day …"

Peter sat back and smiled. Television could hold no fears for him; but of one thing he was quite certain: he would never, as long as he lived, ever go near anything remotely resembling a magic shop.